❀ Created with Vellum

DEFIANT MATE

SMALL TOWN ROMANCE

MYSTIC RIVER SHIFTERS

DELTA JAMES

Dedicated to My Two Best Friends:
Renee and Chris, without whom none of
what I do would be possible and to the Girls,
who bring joy to my life every single day

Acknowledgements:
Editing: Lori White, Creative Editing Services
Cover Design: Dar Albert, Wicked Smart Designs
Proofreader: Melinda Kaye Brandt

KEEP UP WITH DELTA ON SOCIAL MEDIA

Facebook page
Facebook group
Instagram
TikTok
Bookbub
Goodreads
Patreon

Signup for my newsletter and
Get the good stuff...
Each month Delta shares her writing updates, novel releases, exclusive content and some fun personal stories.
Plus - there's often a giveaway!

Thank you!

CHAPTER 1

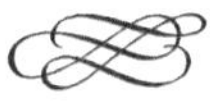

NICOLE

Golden Gate Bridge
San Francisco, California
Two Years Ago

Nicole Sullivan couldn't believe she'd left her vision board for her non-profit client's upcoming gala at home. She thought she'd figured it out in time to catch Kevin, her husband, before he left for his office in the city. Apparently not. His phone kept going straight to voicemail.

Unfortunately, once she'd started across the Golden Gate Bridge, she had to get to the opposite side before exiting the highway and then getting back on to go the other way. Depending on how much time it took her, she might make her meeting on time, but if there was any doubt, she'd call the client.

She wove her way through the busy and narrow streets to reach the townhome she shared with Kevin in the gated community along the bay. Nicole hoped that one day they'd be able to sell and afford to buy one of the famed Painted Ladies. Whenever she had the time, Nicole would drive by them, often stopping to take photos. She understood they were wildly expensive and difficult to obtain, but she knew in her heart she belonged there.

She used her pass to enter through the locked gates and headed to their townhouse. One thing she did like about their home was they had a double car garage and driveway, which meant each of them could park inside.

Kevin had been keen on the three story with the roof deck end unit from the start. Nicole had wanted something with more character but in the end had given in because it wasn't worth arguing about. It never was with Kevin. If he didn't win the argument, he pouted. She wondered if he did that with his court cases.

In the end, she had to agree it was a nice place to live and she did enjoy the community and all it had to offer. They usually only left to go see a play or a concert. Pretty much everything else was within the community walls—grocery store, movie theatre, two swimming pools, two playgrounds, a monitored dog park, an enormous gym, bike paths, and rental boats, as well as every kind of service available from laundry to yard work to housecleaning.

But still… she drove by the Painted Ladies at least weekly. Sometimes she could convince Kevin to go with her, but most times she went by herself and dreamed.

Nicole was a big dreamer. She had dreamed her whole life and then worked her ass off to make those dreams come true. She'd met Kevin at Stanford when he was little more than a year away from graduating law school. Nicole had majored in business and left college with an MBA and an offer for a job in San Francisco working for an elite event company. She'd worked her way up the corporate ladder to become a senior event planner. The days were long, but she enjoyed her work and was never bored.

She and Kevin eloped to Vegas. It was probably the single most exciting thing they'd ever done. Kevin wasn't what one called spontaneous. He studied for the bar while Nicole supported them, and they saved money by living in a third-floor walk-up. When he passed the bar, Kevin received several job offers from firms in the city by the bay and so they'd saved money for a year, purchased a small condo with a great view and then two years ago had upgraded to their current home.

Nicole turned into the driveway and hit the garage door opener, planning to pull into the garage and run inside to get the vision board. As the door opened, the first thing that struck her was that Kevin's Mercedes was still parked in its usual spot. The second thing that drew her attention was the black BMW sports car parked beside it. The same BMW model he'd had brochures for earlier in the year. Had he gone and purchased a new car for himself without telling her?

That would be bad enough, but if he thought his new BMW was going to get her Range Rover's place in the garage, he could think again. Nicole parked, locking her things in her SUV and heading into the house.

The garage was on the ground floor, with a walk up a short flight of steps into the combination laundry and mud room, which also contained a concealed half bath. She trotted up the steps and tried the door into the house, which they always left unlocked. She was surprised to find it wasn't. Nicole found the proper key and opened the door.

"Kevin?" she called as she walked into the open plan main floor. "Kev?"

Kevin came running down the stairs, looking more than a little disheveled wearing only his pajama bottoms. "Nic, what are you doing here?"

"Are you not feeling well?"

"I'm fine. Why are you here?"

"Well, for one thing I live here." She walked over to the back of the couch where the vision board and its case were leaning. "For another, I forgot this. When did you get the Beamer? I thought we agreed not to upgrade our vehicles for another year or two and I certainly expected you to trade the Mercedes in when you did upgrade."

"The Beamer?"

Nicole nodded slowly. "Yes, the Beamer. The black one parked in my spot in the garage. And that's another thing—I'm not giving up my spot. Why didn't you answer your phone? I called a couple of times. I was hoping you could either meet me with the vision board or leave it up at the gate."

"I… I was busy."

"Busy? At home in your pajamas? Busy doing what?"

"I don't need to be subjected to your accusations," he said too quickly and far too defensively.

"Accusations? Interesting choice of words, counselor. You want to tell me what's going on?"

It was at that precise moment her world stopped spinning on its axis as she saw the two champagne flutes with what looked to be the leftovers from mimosas as well as some chocolate dipped strawberries. Nicole hated champagne and was allergic to strawberries.

When she looked from the champagne glasses to Kevin's face, she saw over his shoulder a simply stunning, elegant blonde hesitating at the bottom of the stairs, with a straight chic bob and a perfect body dressed in lingerie that Nicole didn't even want to know the cost of, along with her only sexy dressing gown made out of a gossamer silk.

Nicole walked towards the blonde.

"Nic, this doesn't have to get ugly," started Kevin.

"It doesn't? Yet another thing we'll never agree on." She looked up to engage the blonde, feeling every single one of her excess pounds, shlumpy clothes, and dark curly hair pulled up into a professional messy bun. "I take it he bought you the BMW?" The blonde nodded and she turned back to Kevin. "Tacky, Kev. Using marital assets for your bimbo is kind of a no-no."

"I am not a bimbo," said the blonde.

"Sure, you are," asserted Nicole. "You're screwing my husband in my home in my bed. The BMW he bought you with our community property is parked in my garage and you're standing there in my dressing gown. I'm pretty sure added all together that adds up to bimbo."

"Nicole, I won't have you speaking that way to…"

She wasn't sure who was surprised more by the crack of her hand across Kevin's handsome face. "No," she said shaking her head. "I don't want to know the bimbo's name." She glanced at her cell phone. "I… um… I need to go. I have a meeting with a client who does important work on behalf of the starving children in this country and around the world. Kevin? You and I can talk this afternoon. I should be home by three. Please have the bimbo and her BMW cleared out and see that my dressing gown is picked up by the dry cleaners. Oh, and wash the fucking glasses and plates."

Nicole spun on her heel, almost tripping over her wide palazzo pants, recovering without doing a face plant, picked up her portfolio case and strode from her home with as much dignity as she could muster. Once she was in her car, she looked to see if Kevin had even followed her out, not all that surprised when he hadn't.

Backing out of the driveway, she turned and headed back out of the gated community, calling her assistant at the firm.

"Ang? Can you call Ken Thompson and tell him I'm running late? I forgot the damn vision board. Then I need you to call that lawyer Judith Masters used last year when she got divorced and get me the earliest appointment you can this afternoon."

"Jesus, Nic. You're divorcing Kevin?"

"Yeah. I forgot my vision board and went back for it, only to find a new BMW parked in my spot in the garage as well as champagne glasses, strawberries dipped in chocolate, and some blonde bimbo wearing my favorite dressing gown and lingerie I'm pretty sure he bought her, now that I think about it. There was a huge charge on our credit card. I thought the sonofabitch had remembered our anniversary. Guess I was wrong about that."

"Do you want me to meet you at the client's, or…

I don't know… gather the troops so we can go to your place and kill Kevin?"

Nicole smiled. Ang was the absolute right person to call. Now she just needed to turn on some *Mary Chapin Carpenter* and try to find a calm space while she drove to meet her clients.

"No, I think divorcing his ass, taking at least half of everything, and forcing him to sell that fucking townhouse he loves so much will suffice. I'll give you a call after the meeting."

"I'm on it. Don't forget to call me. In fact, call me when you get there."

"That's not necessary. I'm fine… or, at least, I will be."

"Well, I'm not fine, so call me anyway."

Nicole laughed and turned on *Come On Come On*. It didn't take long for Carpenter's beautiful song *Rhythm of the Blues* to begin to play. Nicole promised herself she'd get to that emotional place where she wanted to be, a place that Kevin had never been. Pulling into the company's parking lot, she turned off her music app and phoned Ang, assuring her that she was fine.

The meeting with Ken Thompson's board, as well as his senior staff, was a resounding success. They had loved all her ideas and she was glad she'd gone back for her visual materials. If nothing else, she now knew what a jackass she'd been married to. How long had it been she'd first seen the brochures for the Beamer? He'd been seeing the bimbo for at least that long.

I probably shouldn't call her a bimbo. She might be a perfectly lovely person. She'd been fucking somebody else's husband, but then again, they didn't know each other. No. I'm going to focus all my energy and ire on that asshole I married. When I've taken everything I can, the bimbo is welcome to anything that's left.

She called the office. "What's the word, Ang?"

"Judith called in a couple of favors with that law firm. They've handled all of her divorces."

Nicole couldn't help rolling her eyes. She'd almost forgotten Judith was on husband number five—a gorgeous polo player who seemed to dote on her, and vice versa.

"Judith's favorite, the one she's used for the last two and who did her prenup with number five, will meet you at Fog Harbor Fish House. She's got a reservation for twelve-thirty, but she said she'll wait until she sees you. She also asked Judith if you liked blue cheese, which I think is a bit weird."

Nicole laughed. "You've never been to Fog Harbor, have you?"

"No…"

"They have the most amazing blue cheese garlic bread made with fresh sourdough, garlic, and Pt. Reyes blue cheese and herbs. It's amazing and just what every curvy girl starting a divorce would want to start lunch with. Tell Judith I love her already."

Nicole made her way into the city and down to Fisherman's Wharf. She parked in the Pier 39 garage, crossing over to Pier 39 and taking the escalator up. When she entered the building, it was as if they'd been expecting her. She was shown immediately to a prime window table where a short woman with a build similar to her own and gray spiky hair stood and greeted her like an old friend.

"Nicole, I'm so sorry we're meeting under these circumstances. I'm Poppy Brinkman. Judith gave me a little information and then told me regardless of what you said, I was to—and I quote—'rip his balls off and shove 'em up his nostrils.'"

Nicole began laughing. That sounded exactly like Judith, the owner and CEO of the company Nicole worked for.

"That's our Judith," Nicole said, starting to feel better than she had all day.

The waiter delivered the blue cheese garlic bread and took her drink order. Nicole wanted to keep her wits about her and ordered a sparkling ginger lemonade.

"So, we know he's a cheating bastard. Now they say that doesn't mean anything in our lovely no-fault state, but I can tell you most of the judges who get our divorce cases don't like a cheater. They don't care if you're getting divorced but do it before you take up with the next one."

For the next two hours, Nicole and Poppy went over the divorce strategy. Poppy made copious notes and just before dessert, she sent them to her legal assistant.

"I'll have the paperwork done before I close up shop for the day. Here's my cell phone and my direct line. You let me know if and when you want to proceed."

"I want to proceed. I know the marriage is over and I can never forgive him."

"Then I'll have the documents sent to you for your signature in the morning. I know he's a shit and he's done you wrong, but still, I'm sorry this has happened to you."

"Thanks, Poppy. At least I feel like I'm in good hands."

Her new divorce lawyer paid the check and gave her a hug before they parted ways.

Nicole headed home. She wasn't sure what to expect when she arrived, but what she got certainly wasn't it.

CHAPTER 2

NICOLE

*N*icole passed through the gate and pulled into the driveway hitting the garage remote. Nothing happened. She pressed the button again. Again nothing. *Maybe the damn battery has run out of juice. Did garage remotes even use batteries?*

She parked her car, got out and headed up to the front door. When she slid the key in the lock, it went in fine, but that was the moment she realized that it was a whole lot more than just the damn garage remote not working. She tried the key again. Nope. Nothing. It would not turn the internal mechanism to open the door. She pounded on the door. Even though she could hear someone moving around inside the townhouse, no one answered. *That asshole!*

Getting back into her car, she dialed Kevin's cell. Straight to voicemail. *Well, no surprise there.* Nicole dialed Poppy's cell number before heading out of the development.

"Let me guess, you can't get into your home?" asked the lawyer before Nicole said a word. Nicole guessed that Poppy already knew the answer.

"Yeah. So now I have to go to a hotel, buy makeup and shit… I'm so pissed."

"Not to worry. I hate to say it, but this isn't uncommon. I'll address it in the paperwork and call the managing partner at his firm. I'll have the SOB served at work. I'm going to make a reservation for you to stay at *Lobo Bahía.* I'll text you the address. It's a small boutique hotel. I'll put it on my credit card. See if yours is still working. My guess is no. Don't let this rattle you. He wants you to think he's in control. He wants you afraid. Don't be, and he isn't. I promise you every shitty thing he does is going to cost him."

"He can't just lock me out of our house and cancel my credit cards."

"Legally? No, and the paperwork and my call to the managing partner will address that. Be prepared for him to have drained the bank accounts, too. Again, don't let him get to you. If he tries to call you? Refer him to me and block his number. All this does is let me know he wants to play dirty. That's okay. I like the mud.

I've used *Lobo Bahía* for cases like this before. We'll make him pay. They have a boutique inside the hotel. I'll have them get together some things for you, as well as their spa line of makeup. You'll love it. Just get comfortable and let them pamper you. If you need me, don't hesitate to call, day or night. We'll get you through this, Nicole, and we'll make the bastard pay."

Feeling a whole lot less frazzled and oddly comforted by Poppy's nonchalant attitude, Nicole began to relax and said, "Thanks, Poppy."

Nicole didn't wonder that Judith used Poppy as her divorce lawyer. Poppy's calm, cheerful demeanor was probably going to be crucial in the next couple of months. Nicole pulled up to the sleek, exclusive hotel. She'd been to dinner at the revolving restaurant on the floor beneath the owner's penthouse but had never been inside the hotel itself.

The parking valet assured her she was expected, and they would make her stay as comfortable as possible. She went inside and found when she tried to transfer the charges to her own credit card that Poppy was right; it didn't work.

"I'm so sorry," Nicole started, feeling embarrassed and as though she needed to explain.

The front desk clerk waved away her concerns. "Not to worry. You aren't the first and won't be the last of Ms. Brinkman's clients to find refuge with us. We'll make your stay as pleasant as possible."

"You're very kind."

"So are you, and you did nothing wrong. Your soon-to-be-ex is a bastard and is about to have his balls cut off and handed to him."

Nicole laughed. "I shouldn't think that's funny or be hoping I'm there when she does it, but I am."

"Write down your sizes, colors you like, and let me know what you need in terms of work attire, lounging around, et cetera. I do recommend a swimming suit. Our pool and hot tub are to die for. We've put you up on the corner of the fifth floor, which gives you a little more room, and it has a beautiful view. I can have some things sent up for your approval. Why don't you let me order some appetizers and your preferred beverage and you can decide what you want for dinner. When you have a minute, look in the mini-fridge and let me know if you'd like us to stock it differently for you."

"Wow," Nicole said impressed. "I can see why Poppy uses you."

"Linc—the owner—is kind of old school in how he treats women—like we're the greatest gift to the world. He is madly in love with his wife, and he and Grace are wonderful to work for. Their whole thing is that we, all of us, are here to serve the guests and make their stay as pleasant as possible."

"Thank you so much. Between you and Poppy, I'm beginning to think I might just come out the other side of this in better shape than I came in."

"That's the spirit. Do you want me to send someone up with you?"

"No, it's just me and my bag and my laptop."

"Do you have your charger with you, and would you like us to set up an additional monitor or two?"

Nicole grinned. In spite of everything, she was starting to believe this might be the best thing that ever happened to her.

"If I could have two external monitors, that would be fantastic."

"If you think you're going to be working in your room a lot, let me have them bring you an ergonomic chair and printer."

"Okay, now, you're just spoiling me."

"Yes ma'am. That's the way we want you to feel."

"Any chance you offer massages?"

"In your room or down on the spa floor?" said the clerk with a smile. "I can set you up with a great spa experience—you sit in the hot tub, then get wrapped in these amazing cotton blankets so that your pores open up and the toxins come out. Then it's an hour-long hot stone massage and a facial."

"Sounds like heaven. As soon as Poppy gets my money situation figured out…"

"No, ma'am. I spoke to her personally and she said anything Nicole wants, Nicole gets, as well as anything you—being me—think she needs. And I think you need some pampering so unless you have plans for Saturday, I'm setting you up. I'll let you know what time. Trust me, it's fabulous. In fact, why don't you just let us take care of you all day."

Nicole sighed. "I could use a day to do nothing but be pampered. It's a date."

She couldn't believe how much better she felt. In fact, she had a sneaky suspicion Kevin was in for a particularly nasty couple of months. *Good.* She left the reception desk with a definite spring in her step.

When she entered the ornate elevator, it was as if she had taken a step back in time. It was gorgeous, purring as it moved up the floors and opened out onto a lush and beautifully decorated hallway, with a sign pointing her to her new digs. Obviously, she couldn't stay here for the duration, but it was awfully tempting.

By the time she got to her room, Nicole wanted nothing more than to hole up in *Lobo Bahía* until the divorce was over. She'd need to talk to Poppy about how long that might be, but she was grateful Poppy had given her such a soft place to land. The hotel was central to everything, and the room was perfect, with its two glass walls providing her a glorious view overlooking the city and bay.

There was an enormous bouquet of fresh flowers in an abstract glass vase, which Nicole was certain was hand-blown. She laughed as she and several of her colleagues had taken a training course on the 'secret language' of flowers. There wasn't a one in the bouquet that didn't mean revenge, new start, hatred and several other less than noble emotions. The choice of the flowers, the extravagant vase and the bold script of her name on the envelope told her who was responsible—her boss, Judith. Nicole opened the envelope.

Sweetie,

Don't let the bastard get you down. I always thought you were way too good for him.

Listen to Poppy and be ready to get in the trenches and fight for what is yours. Do not let that little prick cheat you any more than he has.

Why not work from the hotel and take care of yourself. Everybody here at the office loves you and we've got your back.

Always,

Judith

Nicole kicked off her shoes and wandered into the bath. It was luxurious and appeared to have a steam shower. There was a discreet knock on her door. She left the bath and went to open the door.

"Room service. Denise sent me up to make sure you had everything you need. The chair, printer, and monitors will be up in a few and she wanted you to have some of our appetizers. I brought water as I wasn't sure what you'd like, but there's Diet Coke in the mini-fridge. If you'd like something else, I can send it up with the office equipment."

"Wow, you really take that whole here to serve the guests thing seriously."

"Yes, ma'am, we do. It's one of the things the hotel is known for."

"So, what do you recommend in the alcohol department?"

"If you like peach, our peach sangria is second to none."

"That sounds divine."

"Glass or pitcher?"

"Glass, I have to work tomorrow."

"Glass it is. The room service menu is right here," he said getting it out of the desk drawer. "Let us know if you're dining here, upstairs in the restaurant, or don't want to be bothered."

"Most likely here in my room. It's been… a day."

"We'll try to turn that around for you."

She signed the bill and he left. Nicole went to the mini-fridge and got a Diet Coke and then proceeded to explore the various appetizers that had been sent up. There were some that seemed exotic and that she'd never tried before. Throwing caution to the wind, she decided to try them all.

Another knock on the door, and Nicole opened it to find a whole troupe of people.

"We can come back one at a time, but we have your peach sangria, clothes and make up as well as your office set up."

"The more the merrier," Nicole said, stepping back and gesturing for them to enter. She was going to enjoy her stay at the hotel.

The woman with the ergonomic chair, monitors,

printer and a lovely antique table Nicole thought was probably to hold the printer looked at the desk and room's set up. "Are you going to be doing a lot of work here in your room? If so, I think you'd be more comfortable if we move the desk, so you have a better view."

"I don't want you to go to any trouble…"

"It's no trouble at all."

Nicole took the proffered drink from the room service staff person and then turned to the woman who had a rolling cart loaded with clothes, shoes, and accessories. She and Nicole spent the next hour looking at clothing, sizing, and make-up. Nicole had been promising herself a makeover and this seemed like as good a chance as any.

Before she could make any firm plans, she needed to talk to Poppy about what she could expect in terms of money, getting her things and forcing Kevin from their home, as well. If he thought she would be cowed by his behavior, he was wrong. Like Poppy, Nicole was more than ready to, as Judith's card had suggested, get into the trenches and fight.

As she sat back on the love seat and put her feet up, she decided if Kevin was going to trash their life and embrace a new one with his bimbo, he could. She would do the same—minus the bimbo.

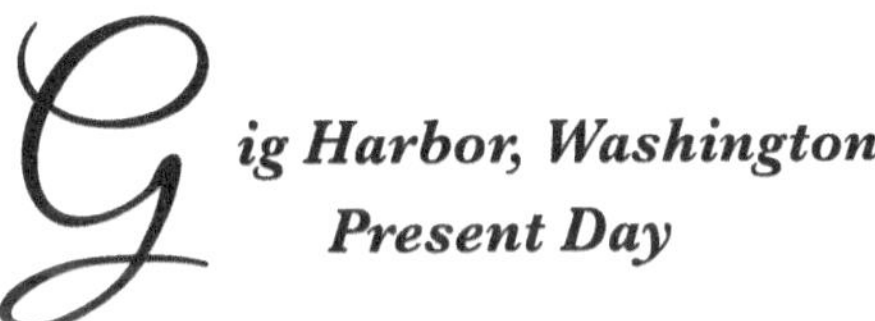

*ig Harbor, Washington
Present Day*

Nicole walked down the community dock to the kayak that she'd reserved.

"Morning, Nicole!" called Pete, who took care of the communal boats, dock, meeting room, and maintained the other common areas.

She raised her hand and waved. "Hey, Pete. How's it going?"

"It's a sunny day in the Pacific Northwest, so it can't be all bad."

Nicole laughed and made her way to the kayak, put on her life jacket, and launched into the water. It felt good to be outside in the sunlight and fresh air.

She doubted anyone remembered that it was the second anniversary of her divorce. It was not a day for mourning or regret as Kevin had predicted, but rather one for celebration and joy.

She'd sent Poppy a bottle of her favorite wine yesterday, as she had the day the divorce was final and on the first anniversary of that day. It had been a hard-fought battle, but they had prevailed. In the end, their assets had been split fairly if not amicably. Nicole still laughed when she remembered the moment Kevin realized all his underhanded tricks had been discovered and the judge had imposed sanctions on him. He'd then been given the choice to come clean about all his hidden assets or be reported to the California Bar Association.

He'd wanted desperately to hold on to the bimbo's Beamer, his own Mercedes, and the townhouse. Poppy had been willing to do that, but he'd had to pay for it through the nose. He'd also racked up incredible legal bills when he'd either fired his attorneys or they fired him. In the end, one of the attorneys from his firm represented him and made him come to the table and finalize the divorce. All in all, because of Poppy, Nicole had come out in good shape—both financially and emotionally.

The divorce had made her really look at herself, her life, and what she wanted moving forward. Nicole felt she'd wasted a lot of years catering to Kevin who had been proven to be a serial philanderer. She'd begun to take better care of herself, losing some weight, but mainly getting in better shape and doing things she'd never done before—kayaking, white-water rafting, hiking, and mountain climbing.

The morning after her divorce, Judith had called and wanted to meet with her and Poppy for breakfast.

She entered the restaurant and spotted the two women who had become her closest friends. Once they ordered their meal, Judith got down to business.

"You know the firm is doing well. And you know we've done three corporate events plus two big weddings up in Seattle," Judith said without prelim-inaries.

"I do. I've really enjoyed working up there," said Nicole, wondering where this was going. Of the five events, she had handled all but one.

"Do you love it enough to leave San Francisco? They love you up there, and I've got people clamoring for our services. I want you to open a satellite office and run it. I'll make you a partner in the firm."

Nicole wasn't British, but the term *gobsmacked* seemed to apply. Judith had built her business from the ground up and was beholden to no one.

"I'm flattered..." started Nicole.

"Don't be. It'll be a hell of a lot of work. I don't want to pressure you, Nic..."

"That's total bullshit," said Poppy. "Of course, she wants to pressure you. She wants you to say yes."

"Whose lawyer are you?" snapped Judith.

"Don't you get snippy with me. I told you I was here as a friend only."

"Here's the deal, I'm a little tight with cash at the moment and I want to open that office. I've got enough for down here, but it would stretch me to open a site in Seattle. I know Poppy got you a good settlement and some of it is cash. I want you to go in on the Seattle office as my junior managing partner. When it proves successful—and I know it will be—you become a partner with a sixty/forty split in my favor and in five years, fifty-one/forty-nine. If you agree in principle, we can have the papers drawn up."

Nicole ran a finger across her bottom lip as she thoughtfully eyed her boss. "Three years and you have a deal. I'm assuming you ran this past our mutual friend who probably told you it was something I can afford to do."

Judith nodded. "She never showed me any numbers. I showed her mine and she agreed, as a friend, it might be worth talking to you about. Split the difference at four years."

Nicole laughed and extended her hand. "Four years it is, partner. The four years starts from the day the firm opens in Seattle."

"We'll do a big event for an open house and announce your partnership that night," Judith said with a smile. "God, this is going to be fun."

"A lot of work, but I think this is just the break I need. I've had more than one passing thought about leaving San Francisco, and the Pacific Northwest was definitely in the mix of places I was considering."

Judith threw back her head and laughed. "Let me guess, you mentioned to our mutual friend here that you were thinking about leaving me." She turned to Poppy. "You are such a bitch."

Poppy lifted her mimosa. "Takes one to know one," she said with a laugh.

"Can your firm handle the paperwork?" asked Nicole. "I know you mostly handle divorces and custody cases."

"We've been handling Judith's business matters for years. Nicole, in all honesty you should get outside counsel to look at it."

Nicole shook her head. "Can't we both sign something that says we just want you to handle it and we are waving any claims of conflict of interest?"

"You can if you want."

"I'm willing if Judith is."

"I am, too," said Judith.

"Then I'll have the papers drawn up by the end of the week. And I will admonish both of you to have outside counsel just look it over."

With that settled, the three friends had proceeded to enjoy their breakfast and talk about the new business venture. Nicole had located office space in Seattle down on the waterfront with a dedicated private courtyard and small event space. The new branch office had been an incredible success from the beginning, and they were now booked up a year in advance.

Nicole chose Gig Harbor for her new home. It was a fast forty-minute commute on the passenger-only hydrofoil and the office was an easy walk from where the ferry docked. Her home wasn't big or flashy but was a planned community of small cottages built around an outdoorsy lifestyle. Nicole loved it.

What her home lacked in size, it made up for in elegance and location. She had a one-hundred-and-eighty-degree view of Puget Sound. The community was small, but the neighbors were all friendly and often entertained as a group. She'd made good friends but had avoided dipping her toes into the dating pool again, even though Judith encouraged her to do so.

Nicole wasn't ready and was beginning to feel as though the problem wasn't that she'd never be ready, but whether or not she actually wanted to. Setting up, promoting, and booking business for the new office; finding and decorating her new home; and figuring out who she was without Kevin and what she wanted in her life had become her focus. A new man was a distant second or third issue to be considered in time.

She loved being on her own...being her own person and not answering to anyone else. Every time she pulled into the driveway of her new home, she realized how much Kevin would have hated everything about the house, Gig Harbor, and her new life. Somehow that made it all a little sweeter.

Nicole made her way out into the Sound, enjoying the gentle sway of her craft as she paddled rhythmically through the water. Pete knew she was out and knew where she planned to kayak, but she was cognizant that although she was on the water by herself, she was not truly alone. Orcas had been sited close to Gig Harbor. Normally, the incredibly beautiful whales were not dangerous if you gave them space and left them alone. She kept her gaze constantly moving to ensure she didn't put herself in dangerous situations.

She had, according to her friends, a bad habit of doing things alone. As she explained to them, her entire work life was built around being with people. She needed time alone to recharge and relax, and often that meant hiking, kayaking, or even climbing by herself. Most of her recent expeditions had been scrambling up some of the more local mountains. Scrambling was a term used to describe the kind of grey area between hiking and technical climbing. It was more intense than just hiking, but usually nothing other than hiking boots and a strong grip was needed.

Technical rock climbing was more intricate and required special gear—including shoes, ropes, ice axes, and the like. Nicole had been working with several instructors to learn how to climb up, down, and across the natural terrain of rock formations and mountains. It was a demanding sport that required the climber to be in top shape both mentally and physically. It tested the climber's strength, endurance, agility, balance, and mental acuity.

So far, she'd been on five technical climbs and had loved the way adrenaline surged through her body and then rushed to an almost climactic level when she reached the summit. Where kayaking relaxed her; rock climbing challenged her. One of her instructors had called her an adrenaline junkie and Nicole wasn't sure she'd disagree.

She'd left the staid, out of shape Nicole back in San Francisco. The new Nicole wasn't the sleek, elegant figure that Judith was. In fact, most would call her curvy. But curvy didn't mean she was unhealthy or unfit. Besides, she liked her curves, and it was far easier to maintain her healthy lifestyle if she wasn't focused on trying to fit into a smaller size than her body naturally wanted her to be.

Nicole relaxed into the rhythm of the kayak. She kept an awareness of her surroundings, finding boaters to be more of a danger than the orcas so many were afraid of, but she allowed her mind to drift. It was as if she could be two separate creatures in one body: her in control, careful self and her wilder, more feral self. The feral side of her being demanded freedom and found solace in solitude. She was feeding that beast today and had begun to consider what to do on her planned vacation.

One of their corporate clients wanted to plan an executive staff retreat up in Alaska and had offered to send her up to scout locations. After talking with Judith, they decided to take the job on. It wouldn't hurt to get their name known up in America's most northern state and it could work well for some of the destination weddings they were considering.

Nicole held the shaft of the paddle as she dipped the blades first on one side and then the other. She moved at a steady pace, slicing through the water almost silently and enjoying the never-ending beauty of Puget Sound. She could see a small pod of orcas in the distance and recognized one of the dorsal fins as an individual she had seen before. The whale seemed almost comfortable with kayakers, but still she turned and paddled in another direction.

She'd been wanting to do a technical solo climb for a while and both she and her instructors felt she was ready. She knew there was no way she was ready to challenge the indomitable Denali or most of the other peaks in the Alaska Range, but one of the towns she wanted to check out was Kodiak, located on the island of the same name. It was home to Pyramid Mountain, which was kind of a baby mountain at not quite twenty-four hundred feet as opposed to Denali, which towered at over twenty thousand.

The thing Pyramid had going for it was that although modest in terms of elevation, it did offer a fairly rugged terrain that Nicole believed might be a better bet for her first solo climb. It had an added degree of difficulty with its isolation and the fact that it was in a subpolar oceanic climate zone.

As she headed back to the dock, she realized she'd made her mind up and would need to pack her climbing gear to take with her to Alaska. Some of the people she climbed with might not even consider the peak a mountain, but the U.S. Geological Service did and that was good enough for Nicole. The only person she tried to impress these days was herself. This seemed like the best candidate for a calculated and cautious first attempt at a solo technical climb.

Pyramid Mountain… here I come!

CHAPTER 4

ASHER

asher Wells drove out from his home in Kodiak to the wilderness at the base of Pyramid Mountain. Because it had neither the elevation nor the reputation of Denali, it was most often overlooked by skiers, hikers, and mountain climbers. Although not overly tall, it still possessed rugged terrain and could be challenging to even the most experienced human.

Finding a place to pull off safely wasn't easy, but Asher parked and then got out. He walked to the other side of his Jeep and removed his clothes, shivering in the arctic air as he folded and locked them inside. He placed his keys in the hidden magnetic container at the top of his wheel well. It was easy enough to get to regardless of whether he was man or beast.

As a man, most found him impressive, if not a bit

intimidating. He wasn't nearly as imposing as Jax Miller, his best friend since childhood and the sheriff of his hometown of Mystic River, north of Kodiak, but was striking in his own right. Well over six feet in height, Ash had a chiseled face, sculpted pecs, and a set of washboard abs. He was muscular in the way most alpha wolf-shifters were and was in top shape. His job as the head of the U.S. Forest Rangers in Alaska meant that not only did his life often depend on his prowess in the wild, but also that of his fellow rangers and those they served.

He closed his eyes and smiled. His wolf had been waiting. It had been more than a month since he'd been able to find the time to allow his more primal self to come out to play. Asher called him forward and the great beast bounded towards him as the swirling, highly charged mist enveloped him and once more man became wolf. Larger than purebred wolves, his lycan self was a mix of tawny and golden tipped hairs with a black mask and white-tipped tail.

Asher shook himself from the tip of his nose to his tail, waggling his head back and forth, shaking his shoulders, body, and hips and wagging his tail as if to reacquaint himself with his other half. He raised his muzzle to the sky and howled, listening to see if anyone might answer. His only response was the bitter wind as it ruffled his fur. It was fast approaching dusk, so he didn't expect to find humans within reach of his call, but this was the time his brethren, both two-legged and four, were beginning to prowl.

Sensing he was alone, Ash bounded away from the Jeep to stretch out and revel in his more primitive state. He ran over frozen ground and icy rock. As a human he'd never be able to move this swiftly and sure-footedly. But for his wolfen self, this was nothing. He jumped fallen trees, making a mental note of ones he and his staff might want to look at removing or at least cutting a path through. Generally, they could find those in need of firewood to keep warm who were willing to come in, cut it up, and haul it away.

The base of Pyramid Mountain was fairly easy to ascend and if it required more than hiking, it was just a minor scramble. This time of year, though, people needed to be wary of brown bears and the occasional Kodiak bear milling around. His friend Jax was one of the latter, or rather, he was a Kodiak bear-shifter.

All of the residents of Mystic River were shifters, and for the most part they at least tolerated one another. It had always been that way in Mystic River. If, somehow a human found their way into town, everyone was on their best behavior until Jax could give them a reason to move on.

His father's pack, the Mystic River Pack, were the last wolves of any kind on the island. Wolves had been hunted into extinction long ago, and wolf-shifters had crossed over to the mainland in search of a better, or at least easier, life. The pack was in danger of extinction due to his father's unwillingness to modernize their way of living. Wolves, especially she-wolves, left in droves in search of a different way of life.

More than once his father had intimated that if Asher would just come home and take over the pack, Ash could institute whatever changes he wanted, and his father would step aside to let him rule. Asher didn't believe that for even a minute. His father had been alpha far too long. There was no way he would peacefully relinquish his role. No, his father had other reasons for wanting him to come home.

Asher had given it some thought when he had left the Navy where he'd spent almost a decade as a SEAL, and then again when he'd been promoted to the head ranger for the ranger service in Alaska. Each time, though, everything in him told him coming home to take his 'rightful place,' as his father called it, was a mistake and that there were dark and dangerous waters there, as well as hidden agendas he was unable to see.

He could easily have lived up in Mystic River and still led the rangers based just outside the city of Kodiak. But the survival instincts that had kept him and his fellow SEALs alive informed him there was something he wasn't being told and that whatever it was could not only be the end of the Mystic River Pack, but Asher himself.

Ash shook his head to clear it of maudlin thoughts and instead listened to the whistling and howling of the wind as he ran along the top of the lower portion of Pyramid Mountain. He loved this place. The mountain was deceptive and to understand it, the climber needed to divide it into thirds. The first part was a moderately difficult hike. The second third, where he was now, started as a difficult scramble and progressed at the midpoint to a technical climb, increasing in difficulty as the climber approached the top third. The last third of the mountain was a difficult technical climb all the way to the summit. The views on a clear day were gorgeous, but more often than not, the peak was shrouded in fog and mist.

He loved the feel of the ground beneath his feet as he made his way around the mountain. It felt good to stretch out and run, his muscles rippling and working in concert with his heart and lungs. In his wolf form he could separate his mental capacity—allowing one part to simply be and experience the ground, the air, the scents, while the other part could either relax or focus on whatever might be bothering him.

He'd talked to Jax earlier in the day. It seemed their old buddy, Colby, was up to his old tricks.

"You know, at some point, you're going to have to arrest his sorry ass," Asher said.

"Me? Why me? Why not you?"

"Because you're the sheriff in Mystic River. I'm just a lowly federal employee, a mere forest ranger…"

"Lowly federal employee, my ass," snarled Jax. Bears and their shifter brothers tended to be bad-tempered. "You're the fucking head ranger for all of Alaska and he does most of his illegal shit on federal land."

Asher laughed. "We might know he's doing it, but so far, nobody's been able to prove it. He's a slippery bastard, our lynx-shifter friend."

"I don't know that he is our friend anymore," sighed Jax, who felt the sting of Colby's cold disdain far greater than Asher did.

"Do you even talk to each other?"

"Oh, we exchange the normal fuck yous, accusations, growling, and snarling. I swear, sometimes I look at him and wonder if somehow what happened didn't break more than just his body. I wonder if they didn't shatter his spirit."

"I don't disagree. But unless and until he's ready to talk or let us help him, there's nothing we can do."

"I know. Occasionally, if there's some kind of celebration going on in town, I'll see snatches of the old Colby. But if he sees me, he turns away and goes back to being the asshole gangster we all know and hate."

"But he leads his clowder and takes care of them, doesn't he?"

"Yeah, that's the weird part. Sometimes I feel like there's a whole lot going on at Windsong nobody outside that clowder knows about. I'm not even sure all of them know about it—whatever it might be."

"Are things any better between him and his sister?"

"No. Kyra can barely stand to look at him. I think she's like you and me. We remember the guy he used to be and wonder what the hell happened to him. Were you ever able to get any information about what happened after they separated him from the unit?"

"Not a thing. That was kind of weird. I was just making general quiet inquiries and was shut down completely. I was told, ever so nicely, by my boss that any further poking around could cost me my job."

"Did you even find out how he was discharged?"

"Nope. Nothing. Weird. I just keep hoping that someday…"

"Me too," said Jax.

Asher did feel for Jax. Asher could mostly push it away and pretend nothing had happened and that Colby had returned the same friend and comrade he had been since they were boys. What he and Jax never admitted to each other was the very real fear that they would never see their friend return to the light. Truth to tell, it was another reason Asher preferred to keep his distance.

After he completed his circuit of the mountain, he returned to his Jeep, padding softly towards it. The last thing he needed to do was to be seen in his wolf form. From a distance, he supposed he might be mistaken for an arctic fox or perhaps a coyote or a wolf. The problem was the latter two were nowhere to be found on Kodiak Island—but most of the tourists and a lot of the locals didn't seem to know that. Even if they were, those explanations would only go so far. First, wolf-shifters were considerably bigger than their pureblood counterparts, and enormous compared to a fox. And no one had ever been able to confirm that coyotes had finally secured a foothold on Kodiak. It was possible, though, as they had finally made their way into the mainland of Alaska as their habitat disappeared in the lower forty-eight and Canada.

Circling the Jeep twice to ensure there were no prying eyes to observe his shift and no predators that might see a human as a viable prey animal, he knocked the magnetic key holder from its hiding spot, springing it open and pressing the button on the key fob to unlock the doors and automatically open the hatch back.

He picked up the keys and holder and trotted to the back. He preferred to spend as little time naked in the arctic weather as possible. He looked up at the stars and gave a last, mournful howl. He wanted to ensure any predator knew where he was and would more than likely stay away.

Asher bade his wolf to relinquish control and grateful for the run, it did so. A man again, he swiftly pulled on his polar fleece hoodie and then his Levi's, sitting on the back bumper to pull on his mukluks and tuck his jeans inside them. Once he was standing, he pulled on his down vest, pressed the key to close the hatchback and got inside the Jeep, turning it on and letting the engine warm up before buckling his seat belt, putting the vehicle in gear, and heading back for Kodiak.

As he passed by the airport, he felt a distinctive buzzing in his head like a thousand fireflies had taken flight. There were no insects in his vehicle, but he brushed at his ear anyway as if to dispel it. That seemed to help, and it didn't bother him anymore. He pulled up to his cabin just on the other side of the city and went inside, making his way in the dark as he retained his wolf's heightened senses.

When he saw the message light blinking, Asher picked up the sat phone issued to him for his job and pressed the button to listen.

"Ash? It's Ray. You may want to come into the office in the morning. We've got an application for a rock climb on Pyramid."

Asher wrinkled his nose. *So what?*

"And in answer to you wondering why I think you should be here? It's for a technical climb by a tenderfoot out of Seattle for her very first solo climb. You know that mountain better than anyone and how many times we have to go get people because they thought it wouldn't be an issue to climb such a small peak. She's very excited."

Ray did a fairly good imitation of an excited girl for the last sentence. Probably not politically correct, but funny, nonetheless. Ash hated to admit it, but Ray was probably right. Pyramid Mountain might not be Denali, but it wasn't one of downtown Seattle's seven hills either.

Grabbing a quick bite—and he thought raw steak qualified—he headed into his bedroom so he could take a shower and go to bed. The cabin wasn't large, but it was warm and comfortable and met his needs. One bedroom with an attached bath was fine for him. He was, after all, a lone wolf. He didn't do a lot of entertaining. In fact, he avoided it. If he needed to socialize, he did it in town so that when he chose to be done, he could leave.

Other than the separate bedroom, the rest of the cabin was open living space with a kitchen separated from the rest by a large island. He smiled. As rustic as his cabin might seem to those few who ventured out to meet him, it was nothing compared to the cave Jax preferred to live in. At the other end of the spectrum was Windsong Manor, the stately mansion and land belonging to Colby, or his father's sprawling estate, Wolf Run.

He stood in the shower looking down at his dick, which seemed to be in need of some attention. Much better to have that of a woman, but there wasn't one handy and he wasn't inclined to get dressed, go back into town, and find one. He thought about masturbating but that seemed like too much trouble. Instead, he cut off the hot water and let the icy cold convince his cock that tonight was not a night for play, but instead one for sleep.

After toweling off, he wandered back into the kitchen to get his sat phone and a piece of toast. The latter made him chuckle as he would eat meat raw, but the idea of bread without toasting it first was repugnant. Grabbing the phone and a bottle of cold water, he headed back into his bedroom. Placing the sat phone and water on the bedside table, he turned down the bed, polished off his toast and crawled under the covers. Ash was dead to the world, so to speak, in a matter of minutes.

He often wondered if his old friend slept as easily.

The following morning, Asher felt the buzzing for a second time as he parked his Jeep in front of the ranger station. Maybe he was coming down with something, although that didn't seem likely. Other than the buzz and a brief flash of disorientation, he felt fine.

He opened the door to see Ray trying to explain to the woman with her back turned toward him, and perhaps the finest ass that had ever filled out a pair of jeans, why she didn't want Pyramid Mountain to be her first solo technical climb.

He glanced up with palpable relief as Ash entered. "Ms. Sullivan, this is my boss Ranger Asher Wells. He grew up here on Kodiak and is the head ranger for all of Alaska."

"Fine. Maybe he'll understand why there is no good reason to deny me my permit."

She turned around to face him and he felt as though all of the oxygen had been sucked out of the room. There, standing before him, was the one thing he had never expected to find, much less find this morning arguing with one of his fellow rangers.

His.

The awareness blotted out every other rational, reasoning thought in his head and he had to tamp down on the primal alpha wolf instinct to growl at Ray to get away from her and just toss her over his shoulder, take her back to his place, and claim her as his. He refrained from doing so, reminding himself that the U.S. Ranger service and most people would frown on that sort of behavior.

It was a supreme struggle, though, as it would seem the fair Ms. Sullivan was none other than his fated mate.

CHAPTER 5

NICOLE

*N*icole turned around, ready to argue with whoever this Asher Wells was. She hadn't traveled all this way and lugged all of her climbing equipment out with her to have some local yokel tell her she couldn't climb a mountain that wasn't even half a mile high.

True rock climbers who wanted to ascend the likes of K-2 or Everest or even Denali itself would scoff at the notion that such a peak could even be considered a mountain. For Nicole, Pyramid Mountain was a goal she had set for herself and no ranger who knew nothing about her was going to get in her way.

Spinning on her heel, she came face to face with the most startling, ruggedly gorgeous man she'd ever seen. He might not appeal to some women—his nose was a bit too aquiline, and his eyes set perhaps a bit too closely, but to Nicole he was arrestingly beautiful.

His strong brow and jaw were offset by high cheek-bones. He had a closely cropped beard and hair that had been artfully cut and looked like the wind had been told it could only blow it into a style fit more for New York or Chicago than the wilds of Alaska. And yet, the rugged, muscular build—broad shoulders tapering down to hips attached to what she guessed were muscular thighs—seemed perfectly adapted to his surroundings.

Nicole hoped there was no way he could know that her imagination had been set free, as she could easily imagine his strong, large hands holding and molding her body to his. He'd rolled up his sleeves to reveal thickly corded, muscular forearms. The rest of his body had to match, right? She could picture his strong, sculpted chest and washboard abs. He would have to have those wonderful hip notches that directed a mate's attention to a sizeable cock.

Mate? Where the hell had that thought come from?

His dark eyes withheld whatever was going on behind them. His tanned face was lean, but the easy smile seemed to soften it. It was easy to see the crinkles left by laughter and pain around his eyes, but his beard hid those around his mouth. He was dressed completely appropriately, yet his ranger uniform led her to fantasies of what it would be like to uncover the ripped physique she was certain she would find there. In short, the man was a hunk.

"Ms. Sullivan, I'm Ranger Wells. First, welcome to Alaska…"

Nicole had to fight hard not to just puddle at his feet and do whatever he wanted. What she wanted was now her priority in life and what she wanted was to take her first solo technical climb on Pyramid Mountain. No park ranger, despite how gorgeous he was, was going to stop her. Oh, if he wanted to fulfill the fantasies that continued to grow more sexually explicit by the minute, he might delay her, but he wasn't going to stop her.

"Thank you. Your ranger here seems to think he has a basis for denying me a permit," said Nicole, trying desperately to appear cool, collected, and unaffected by the dark and brooding Ranger Asher Miles.

"There isn't a permit, per se…"

"Good. Then I'll be on my way…"

As she moved to walk past him, he quietly stepped in front of her. "Just because there isn't a permit required doesn't mean that you should underestimate the degree of difficulty involved. More than one novice has ended up needing to be rescued off the side of the mountain."

"According to most, Pyramid barely qualifies as a mountain," she retorted.

She flushed at his proximity and tried to discreetly fan herself. Why was he making her feel this way?

Maybe it wasn't all that surprising. After all, she'd been on her own for a while and the man looked like he'd just stepped off the cover of one of the steamy romance novels she enjoyed reading.

Her favorite author was Maddie Owen, who wrote paranormal tales of beings that could shift from beast to man and back again, with no one knowing of their existence. The books were fun and fantastical and pure escapism. They had enlivened many a lonely night and helped her find her own way. Nicole had been inspired by the heroines in the books who refused to give up until they had their own happy ending.

Nicole hadn't found hers yet, but she was working on it and no park ranger, who knew nothing about her, was going to tell her that she couldn't do something her instructors, who knew her abilities, told her she was capable of doing. Screw that. She was set on expanding her horizons and that meant doing what she felt capable of, not what others deemed appropriate for her.

"I assure you Ms. Sullivan, Pyramid Mountain would present far more of a challenge than you might imagine if you're foolish enough to try it alone. Oh, the lower part isn't too bad, if you can manage to avoid the bears. The middle part requires a lot more scrambling than just hiking and you need to be prepared for ice and arctic winds. *If*, and I think that's a fairly big *if*, you make it up onto the top third, much less manage to get to the summit, you're going to need full-on mountaineering gear, including rope, mountaineering boots, crampons, ice axes, a helmet, a harness…"

"You know, Ranger Wells, it's not like I'm coming up here with no clue as to what to do. All of my instructors think I'm perfectly capable and so do I. Now, if you'll excuse me…" she said as she tried to move past him.

The operative word was 'tried,' as he merely stepped into her path again.

"Do any of these so-called *instructors*," he managed to sneer the word, "have any experience in Alaska?"

"One of them came on an expedition a couple of years ago to try and summit Denali."

"As you say 'try,' my guess is they failed. Might it be the one five years ago led by Don Dodge where one person was killed in a fall, another barely made it after he was airlifted off the side of the mountain, and the other four had to be rescued and brought down by members of our rescue squad?"

Nicole remembered her instructor had mentioned a man named Dodge and that it had been, according to him, gnarly.

"He said they had an unusual amount of bad luck."

Wells snorted. "Their bad luck was they followed an idiot and none of them knew what the fuck they were doing."

"I'm not proposing to try and summit Denali."

He laughed. "That's good because I doubt you'd

make it to base camp. Look, Ms. Sullivan, I'm not trying to be an asshole…"

"Really? Because you're doing an awfully good job for someone who isn't trying. It must just come naturally to you."

The park ranger shook his head. "I'll bet if I asked him, your man would say you're a handful."

Nicole drew herself up, stiffening. Of all the misogynistic… It was a good thing this jerk was good-looking, because he didn't have a lot going for him personality-wise. "I don't have a man, Ranger Wells. I kicked his sorry, cheating ass to the curb a little over two years ago."

They seemed to be at a standoff. It was obvious he didn't want her to go, but he had no legal way to stop her, which meant she was going.

"I'm sorry your ex did that to you. No woman should be subjected to that. I get it if someone wants to leave a relationship, but they exit before they find a new partner. Any man who doesn't has no honor and isn't worthy of a woman like you."

She narrowed her eyes in disbelief. Now, after insulting her abilities that he knew nothing about, he was trying to flirt with her? She stifled a laugh. He really was just like one of Maddie's heroes—dark, dominant, over-protective and hot, hot, hot! But she hadn't traveled all the way here to have a wild fling with a park ranger. She had come, first and foremost, on behalf of the company to look at and secure potential venue spots for events. But she'd also come to climb Pyramid Mountain.

"Thanks, but…"

"I'll tell you what, were you planning to try today?"

"No. I was planning to summit tomorrow."

"Good. Then why don't you check in with one of our local hiking and climbing shops and meet me for lunch at the Black Bear Diner, which is an odd name because we don't have black bears, but the food is good." She hesitated. He was definitely flirting with her. "My treat."

"Only if I can pick your brain about some locations my company is thinking about using, and we'll go Dutch."

"You are going to be a handful, aren't you?" he said with a smile. "The diner is easy to find and most everyone in Kodiak knows where it is. How about we get there a little ahead of their lunch rush, say quarter to twelve?"

"Okay, but you're not going to talk me out of my solo climb."

"We'll have lunch and talk about it." He stepped aside and opened the door for her. "I'll see you at the diner."

"Fine, but you're not talking me out of my climb."

"We'll see."

Nicole rolled her eyes and walked past him. The buzzing in her head that had been so prevalent in the rangers' office seemed to dissipate the further she got away from it. She decided Ranger Wells' advice to talk to one of the local climbing shops wasn't the worst idea she'd heard. She Googled climbing shops and found that for a small city with a population of less than six thousand, there were several to choose from. She decided on To the Top, which had not only the most ratings, but the best ranking overall.

She plugged in her cell phone and followed the navigation unit's directions to the shop. The shop looked as if it had been there forever and imitated a rustic log cabin. Once inside she smiled and felt at home. It was definitely for the more serious climber and seemed to have everything anyone could need.

It was set up the way she thought most trading posts might have been. There was one enormous space with two curtained exits on either side of the long, polished counter. Behind the counter were various and sundry smaller and more expensive items. Nicole thought it was a shame that shoplifting had become so prevalent that even here in remote Kodiak shop owners needed to minimize the opportunity for thieves to prosper.

"Morning, ma'am. How can we help you?" asked the clerk behind the counter.

"I'm planning to get to the top of Pyramid Mountain tomorrow. I was told I ought to check out one of the local climbing stores. I saw your shop on Google and was impressed by the number and high ranking of your reviews."

"We take a lot of pride in helping customers get just what they need. Do you have anything specific in mind?"

"No, I basically planned to kill some time wandering around your store and then meet someone for lunch, but I have to say this is like nirvana." The clerk laughed. "I don't need them, but I couldn't help notice the matching ice axe and ice tool you have on the wall."

"You have a fine eye for design and function. I have a local blacksmith who makes them. He'll do custom orders and ship them, but sometimes he does a set that just speaks to him, and he offers them through the store. Would you like me to get them down?"

She could see the price. They were outrageously expensive, but they were also works of art.

The clerk chuckled. "I know what you're thinking, but Max makes sure they can do the job. He just thinks equipment can be beautiful *and* functional."

"I was thinking how pretty they'd look angled over my mantle where I have my television."

"I'm not trying to push you because I know they're expensive…"

"Don't you want to sell them?"

"Of course, and I will. Max brought them in yesterday. I won't have them by the end of the weekend. For one thing, I have a number of people who love to know when Max brings in items, but what I was going to say is you won't find a better balanced, better crafted pair of tools for the ice anywhere. Max is the best. Let me get them for you."

He brought them down and from the moment she picked the first one up, Nicole knew she had to have them. She looked up at him and grinned.

The bell over the door jangled and two burly young men barely old enough to drink legally in Alaska entered. Their gazes lit on the axe set and brightened with interest. "Whoa! Are those some of Max's?"

"Yes."

"Cool, I want to see," the young man said reaching for the ice axe.

Nicole laid her hand possessively on the handle. "I'm afraid you'll have to wait for the next set. These are going home with me. These are my present to myself for climbing Pyramid Mountain."

"Lucky dog," he said with good humor. "His stuff is amazing."

He and his friend went to another part of the store to look at helmets.

"You're going by yourself… to the top?" asked the clerk.

Nicole's body began to tense in response to another person wanting to dissuade her.

"Yes. I thought it would make a good first solo technical climb."

He nodded. "Ambitious. Pyramid is deceptive, but I salute your chutzpah. Do you have good crampons?"

"I have a set of G-10s."

"Then let me show you the Petzl Lynx. In my opinion, there are none better."

"I've read all about them but just haven't wanted to spend the money."

He picked up a pair and handed them to her. "My gift. If you're spending the money on Max's ice axe and ice tool, you don't want half-assed crampons."

"Are you sure?"

"You bet."

Nicole completed her purchase, which included handmade leashes for each of her new purchases. The crampons didn't need them, but she was glad to have them. She made sure to ask if they did shipping to the lower forty-eight, and was glad to hear they did.

Glancing down at her watch, Nicole realized she had some extra time to drive out of the city and see the countryside. As she drove, her cell rang. Without thinking she hit the answer button on the Jeep's steering wheel, part of the hands-free communication system.

"Nicole? It's Kevin. We need to talk."

"Kevin, how the hell did you get my new phone number? I don't want to talk to you."

She ended the call. Poppy had heard rumors that Kevin was in free-fall. The bimbo had up and left him for a bigger fish at his law firm and he was not moving up the partnership track as fast as he would have liked.

The phone rang again. This time she looked, unsurprised when it was Kevin again. When she didn't answer on the third call, he must have gotten the message. She found a turn-out spot and called Poppy.

"Having fun up in the big freeze?" Poppy answered the phone.

Poppy had lived in California all her life. Her idea of cold was anything colder than San Francisco's temperate climate.

Nicole didn't waste time on trivialities. "I just got a call from Kevin."

"Your ex? How'd he get your number?"

"I have no idea."

"Hmm… that's not good. I'm assuming you don't want to speak with him."

"Oh, hell to the no. I don't even want to know what prompted his call."

"No problem. Let me see if I can find out what's going on. Just block his number and don't talk to him again."

"Will do. Thanks, Poppy."

As she turned the Jeep around and headed back into town, she wondered why Kevin would call her and sound upset and a bit desperate. The last time they'd had any interaction at all, he'd made vague threats. She wasn't actually afraid of him, but if he was on the verge of losing more than the bimbo, that would account for his desperation. He couldn't really think she owed him anything or that she'd so much as lift a finger to help him, could he? If he did, then he was crazy.

A little voice in the back of her mind reminded her that crazy, desperate men could be dangerous. She shook her head to dispel the notion. There was nothing dangerous about Kevin… was there?

CHAPTER 6

ASHER

sher and Randy went over the morning's reports and talked about some upcoming personnel changes in the rangers who served in Alaska. Technically, Randy wasn't any higher grade than the rest of them, but Asher had found him to be good company, steady in the field and able to keep things to himself.

"You were kind of hard on Ms. Sullivan earlier. Are you really going to have lunch with her?"

"I am. And I wasn't overly hard at all. You and I both know Pyramid Mountain is a much harder peak to summit than people, especially those from the lower forty-eight, give it credit for. How many people have we had to go up after? And I don't think she has the kind of experience she needs to solo anything in Alaska."

"You could be right. Do you think you'll talk her out of it?"

"I don't know. She's right, though; legally we can't do anything about it. But I plan to give it my best shot. And I'll find a way to get her to take an emergency beacon."

"You think she'll take it?"

"I don't know. I don't know that she likes taking orders, or even suggestions, from men."

"I hate when a guy does a woman wrong and she wants the rest of us to pay for it."

Asher nodded. "I get that, but I also get if your spouse cheats on you that's a truly egregious violation of your basic trust. I think it would make anyone question whether or not they could ever trust anyone again."

"I suppose, but still."

"Don't worry about it, Randy. I'll look after Ms. Sullivan."

"You will, will you?" Randy said, an enormous smile splitting his face.

"I will, and you can wipe that shit-eating grin off your face."

Realization made Randy's eyebrows raise. "Whoa, you're serious about her."

"I am, and if I don't leave now, I might be late. And that's the last thing I want to be."

Asher left the station and headed towards the Black

Bear Diner. He also wanted to do a little window shopping and see if he could find a little something to give her at lunch. He thought about flowers, but she wasn't from here and he had no way of knowing how long she'd be staying. Besides, Nicole didn't really impress him as a flowers kind of girl. If she hadn't done a lot of ice climbing, though, she might be underestimating the glare of the ice and snow combined. Maybe he'd run by Joe's place, To the Top, and see what he had.

As he passed the only jewelry store in town, he was tempted to stop. But he didn't need everyone in Kodiak knowing he'd been looking at rings. Instead, he continued with his original plan and stopped in to see Joe.

"Hey, Ash. Good to see you," called Joe from behind the counter.

He looked at the place behind the counter where Joe displayed Max's equipment, when Max felt called to a design that wasn't a custom order. Asher did enough technical climbing and when he'd seen them yesterday, he'd been tempted. The blades had glistened, and Ash knew they would be sharp. Max was a master craftsman. The hand-forged handle was red with an intricate design of black wolves. The ice axe and the ice tool were works of art.

"You sold Max's wolves?" he asked.

"Yes, just this afternoon. Nice gal, but I think she's underestimating Pyramid. I gave her a pair of the Petzl Lynx crampons as a bonus."

Asher nodded. "I'm having lunch with her in a bit and am going to try and talk her out of a solo climb. I don't think she's ever climbed up here in Alaska, and I worry her goggles won't be up to the task. What do you have." Joe grinned and he shifted his stance. "Don't start."

"I have a number to choose from, but given her new ice axe and tool, I'd go with the Smith I/0 Mag —the lenses are mirrored and what they call sun red. Highly rated, good value for the money, but if this is a first date, they ain't cheap."

"That's okay. I'm hoping this lunch will lead to better and more long-term things."

"Whoa! You mean the lone wolf is looking to not be so alone anymore?"

Asher rolled his eyes. "Shut up and give me the damn goggles."

Joe laughed. "Shall I put them in a gift box with a pretty bow?" he teased.

"No, a bag will do just fine," he said shaking his head and paying for them.

As Asher headed out, he had no doubt that the fact that he'd purchased a pair of spendy goggles for a tourist would be all over town by sundown. He ducked his head and grinned as he realized, he really didn't care.

Part of what he'd done this morning was find where she was staying and her first name. Nicole. Nicole Sullivan. It was a solid, no-nonsense kind of name. Not exactly the kind of information the hotel would normally give out, but one of the desk clerks was a she-wolf he'd helped leave his father's pack and Ash had assured her he had no nefarious plans. Nicole was a partner in an event planning company with offices in Seattle and San Francisco.

He walked into the diner and waved to the owner, Rick.

"Any place you find space," he called to Asher.

Ash was early and he had beat the rush so picked his favorite booth in the back that overlooked the harbor on the Gulf of Alaska.

"Just you today, Ash?" asked the waitress.

"No, I'm meeting a friend. I'll keep watch for her when people come in, but she should be here about quarter to twelve."

"Good enough. Coffee?"

"That'd be great. The dark roast, please."

The same buzzing that had plagued him previously in the day began again in earnest. He ignored it and tried to suppress the sense of urgency and excitement he felt about having lunch with her. It was, after all, just lunch. Right on time, he looked up as Nicole entered the diner. Asher stood and motioned to her. The buzz and slight sense of disorientation calmed when her eyes caught his, and she smiled. The restaurant was filling up, but it seemed that all he could see was her.

"I thought you were kidding about a lunch rush."

"Rick does a great job. Good food and terrific service at a great price. It's not much on atmosphere if you're looking for romance and ambiance, but it's lively and friendly and they have karaoke on the first Thursday of every month."

"You're kidding," she laughed. "That's one of the less adventurous things on my bucket list."

"You have a bucket list?"

"Sure, don't you?"

"No, I always kind of thought it would be for things when I retire."

"Why wait until you might be too old to really enjoy some of what you want to do?" She picked up the menu. "What's good?"

"I'm told the salads are good, but I love a good meatloaf and can't make one to save my life. I go back and forth between the grilled meatloaf with mashed potatoes and gravy or the grilled meatloaf sandwich. The fish and chips are fresh, hand breaded, and will spoil you for anything else. And sometimes if they had prime rib as a special the night before and there's any left over, they make a French dip sandwich with caramelized onions and gruyere cheese that'll knock your socks off. They had prime rib last night and they currently have their prime rib sandwich, but it won't last the lunch hour. Their soups of the day vary but are always good. They have great clam chowder, and their chili is amazing, but it's hot. Not for the faint of heart."

"Eat here a lot?"

"Probably more than I should. I'm not much of a cook. Give me meat and a fire and I can keep you from starving, but not much more than that. So, I usually stop in on my way home. They also have some pretty amazing desserts. My personal favorite is the carrot cake."

"Blech, I hate raisins and most carrot cake has raisins."

"Ah, then you're in for a treat. Not a raisin in sight; plus, it has pecans and coconut. Heaven on a plate."

"That sounds delicious, but I probably shouldn't."

"Sure, you should. There's nothing wrong with indulging now and again."

She looked up at him, smiling. Nicole had a beautiful face, coal black hair the color of a raven's wing and startling blue eyes with a fair complexion. But when she smiled, it lit up her face and just radiated joy.

"I'm with you about meatloaf, except I do make a good one. I just haven't lately as it seems kind of sad for just one person and most of my weekday lunches are client-related. I can't decide between a meatloaf sandwich or the prime rib French dip."

"I'll tell you what, let's order one of each and we can split them. Do you like fries or onion rings?"

"Depends on the fries..."

"Hand-cut crinkle style and fried so they're crispy

on the outside and soft on the inside and the rings are hand-cut and hand-dipped in a homemade beer batter."

"Let's get one of each and we can split that, too."

"Sounds like a plan. What are you drinking?"

"Diet Coke. I know… diet drink with fattening food."

"I think you should drink what you want."

The waitress came and Asher ordered, more pleased than he should be when she offered to bring them extra plates and Nicole told her not to bother, they'd just share. Things were going much better than he'd thought they might.

"Me, too. Sorry, sometimes I get a little defensive. My ex used to tell me I needed to lose some weight and the bimbo I found him with was built like a barbie doll, which is fine for a doll, not so much for a woman. Oh, God," she said shaking her head. "Listen to me go on. I am trying so hard not to drag what happened with Kevin into my future, but he called me today and it just kind of rattled me."

"Anything I should be concerned about or let the cops know about?"

"No, Kevin's down in San Francisco. I don't think he even knows Alaska is a state, much less how to get here."

Asher laughed. "I think there are a lot of people who still question whether Seward's Folly was just that."

"Not me. Coming up here was one of the things on my bucket list."

"What else?"

"Learning to mountain climb. Learning to white water kayak. I've been sea kayaking for years, but white water in general fascinates me."

"I always think of it as a wet roller coaster."

Nicole nodded. "I invited my boss to come white-water rafting with me. She looked down her patrician nose—don't get me wrong, she's also a good friend—and said, 'I don't like cold water; I don't like roller coasters; what on earth makes you think I'd enjoy that?' I have to admit, she had a point. I've been trying to do things I never thought I'd want to do."

"Like what?" he asked.

"I want to go zip lining in Belize."

"Belize in particular, or just zip lining?"

"I think Belize because you do it over the tops of trees. It just looks like so much fun."

"You're a bit of a daredevil, Ms. Sullivan."

"Please call me Nicole. I'm sorry if I came off a bit frosty earlier."

"Bad divorce from a cheating spouse? I imagine after that it's hard to hear something you don't want to hear from some guy you don't know."

"A little, but honestly, Asher, I do know what I'm doing. Besides I got some new equipment to try out. I took your advice and found one of the climbing stores. It's called To the Top."

"I'm aware. I went in there, as well. I understand you bought Max's latest creations. They were gorgeous."

"I've never seen anything like them."

"And you never will. You'll use them and when your body tells you you're done doing that kind of thing, you can look at them and remember the fun you had. I really think you climbing Pyramid by yourself tomorrow is a mistake, and it's not because I doubt your ability. You just don't know Alaska. To say our weather is mercurial is putting it mildly, and they say we should be bracing for an icy storm from the north."

"I've been in storms before."

The waitress set down their food and he arranged it so it was between them.

"But not an Alaskan storm. Just tell me you'll think about it." He pulled out an emergency beacon. "And if you decide to go anyway, promise me you'll take this. That way if something happens, we'll have a better chance at getting to you in time."

Nicole took the beacon and slipped it into her bag.

"And since I figured I wasn't going to talk you out of it, I got you something from Joe's."

He pulled out the bag and handed it to her. She removed the goggle case from the bag and opened it. Her eyes widened. "It's too much and I have sunglasses."

"Which really aren't going to cut it on Alaskan ice. I think you'll like the difference when you try them, and I won't be worried you'll go snow blind."

She sat back thoughtfully. "You'd be worried?"

"Yes. In fact, if you could wait a few days, I'd be happy to go with you."

"The point of going was to do my first *solo* climb. And I have to leave the day after tomorrow."

"I understand. I don't like it, but I understand. Maybe I can get Randy to switch days off with me…"

"Again, the point of the trip…"

"Okay. How about if you take the goggles, call me when you leave your car and then call when you get safely down the mountain?"

She nodded. "They're red," she said happily.

"They match your new equipment."

They ate their lunch, exchanging bits and pieces of their lives. Nicole was fascinated with his life coming from a small town and then being a SEAL. As they talked, he realized she was a fan of Maddie Owen's books.

"I know this might sound weird, but she writes so well that you can almost believe wolf-shifters exist…"

Asher was well aware of Maddie Owen. She was the fated mate to Griffin Owen of Bae Diogel. Maddie had once been human but had agreed to be turned so she could be one with Griffin. More than once the Ruling Council had thought to move against them or impose sanctions for what they felt was her risking that the truth would become well known. The problem was that Griffin was part of a powerful coalition in the shifter world and no one had been willing to take them on.

It occurred to him that taking Nicole to mate might not be as difficult as he supposed. It sounded as if the idea of fated mates, being turned, and becoming a wolf-shifter had some appeal. And if the concept was not totally appealing, then at least she might not be completely turned off by the idea.

Other wolves had started with less than that; perhaps there was a way to convince Nicole to stay a bit longer. When she excused herself to use the restroom, Asher texted Randy, saying he was taking the afternoon off, but would be available by phone.

When Nicole returned to the table, she glanced around looking for the bill. It was nowhere to be found. "You're not going to let me pay half."

He grinned. "No. I'm sneaky like that."

"Well, two of us can be sneaky, Ranger Wells," she teased.

"Sneaky is fine; it just often has consequences you may not like."

"Well, thank you for lunch and for the goggles. I really shouldn't keep them, but I've been wanting to get a pair."

"If you don't have plans for the afternoon, might you consider spending it with me?"

Nicole paused as she was rising to leave, and sat back down. "I would," she said slowly.

"Any chance an airboat ride along an Alaskan waterway might be on your bucket list?"

"No. Should it be?"

"Absolutely. It just so happens that I own an airboat and know the perfect river. It might be a little rough for some, but if you like white water, I think you'll love it."

"Sounds great. If you're sure I'm not imposing?"

"You're not. Let's drop your car and stuff at my cabin; then we'll pick up the airboat and head out."

"You're on."

They headed out to their respective vehicles and Asher led her towards his cabin. He was sure she had no idea what he was actually leading her toward: a new destiny. All he had to do now was figure out how to keep her off Pyramid—or at least find a way to keep an eye on her to keep her safe—and how to introduce the idea that fated mates and wolf-shifters were real.

CHAPTER 7

NICOLE

*A*sher proved to be not only good company but an excellent airboat pilot. Nicole couldn't remember a time she'd laughed and screamed so much or had nearly as much fun. She hoped that as he saw she could handle things physically he became less worried about her climb tomorrow.

The airboat was a unique experience and one Nicole determined she'd want to do again and again. She asked all kinds of questions about piloting them, maintaining them, and the other things she'd need to know if she wanted to acquire one—or at least enough to begin research about it. Once he realized why she was asking, he offered to start teaching her how to handle the boat. It was so much fun, and much more nuanced than any other kind of boating experience.

"Oh, my god!" she exclaimed as the boat spun around and Asher laughed.

"That's an airplane engine and propeller you've got back there. It's a far more responsive craft. Even a jet ski can't compare. They're quick and maneuverable, but they don't have the horsepower an airboat does."

She nodded. "I've been thinking about getting a jet ski, but after this—no way. This is way more fun, and you can take people with you."

"I've ridden both and I think the airboats are more maneuverable and honestly easier and safer to operate."

"Providing you don't have a klutz at the controls…"

"You are anything but a klutz."

"Yeah?" she said, looking into his eyes.

She could feel the moment things changed between them. What had started out as a lighthearted romp had become, almost immediately, something more serious, something more than she wanted or was ready for. The vehemence of her response this morning was proof of that.

Asher and Randy had done nothing more than express their concern for her well-being. From their point of view, she knew nothing. She knew differently, but instead of trying to explain, she'd just assumed they were putting her down. Too many times rescuing too many people who didn't understand this magnificent country in which they lived made them cautious.

"Yeah," he said, letting the boat idle and cupping the nape of her neck. He pulled her forward, and as his mouth hovered over hers, he said, "Don't go back to Seattle. Stay the weekend. Stay with me."

Before she could answer, his lips came down on hers, nibbling at them until they parted, and his tongue could sweep into her mouth. Nicole clung to him, letting her softness sag against the hard planes of his chest as she moaned. His hand left her neck as his fingers came up to fist her hair and he deepened the kiss, his other hand wrapping around her and holding her close. Nothing had ever felt as good as Asher kissing her. Nothing.

He stood between her legs as she sat in the pilot's seat. Nothing about the way Asher kissed, though, said she'd ever truly be in control where he was concerned. He pulled her against him. Even though there were layers and layers of clothing between them, she could feel his dick hardening against her as her nipples stiffened and pushed against the constraints of her bra.

Asher nuzzled her neck when he finally relinquished her mouth, inhaling her scent and whispering. "God, you smell sweet."

"It's just the hotel soap."

What a stupid thing to say!

"That's not the scent I was referring to, Nicole. Your arousal is the sweetest scent I've ever known."

She laughed a bit nervously, not knowing quite how to respond. And then his mouth came back to hers and there was nothing for her to say, as there was no way to say it. She let her arms explore as much of his body as she could under his clothing. Sure, there was the softness of the down and the multiple layers. But beneath them he was as solid as the mountains that had spawned him.

When he tugged her head back and trailed kisses from her mouth to her jaw and back down her throat, Nicole moaned and tried to get closer. His hand tugged at the hem of her sweater and suddenly his warm hand was on her naked skin. Nicole tried to return the caress, and he pulled away, shaking his head.

"Not like this. I want you alone, naked, and in my bed."

There it was. He'd declared, in no uncertain terms, what he wanted.

"If that's not what you want, I need to know. If I'm rushing you, I need to know that, too."

Nicole had vowed to herself when she moved to Gig Harbor that fear would no longer be the determining factor in her decision-making process. She pressed herself against him.

"I want you, too, and I don't feel pressured or rushed. I'm not sure what this might be, but I know I don't want to leave on Friday and always wonder what if…"

Asher smiled. "It's a good thing you want it, too. I'm not sure what I would have done if you didn't."

"Really?" she teased.

"Okay, so I would have figured out a way to get you into my bed and never let you go."

Asher broke away and moved her from the pilot's seat, so he had the controls. He spread his legs and made a place for her to sit with him. They raced down the river to the launch point and brought the boat out of the water, then headed back to Asher's cabin.

Once inside, they came together in a way that was new and exciting and yet felt as though they had done this a thousand times before. The buzzing was back, but now it was more like a hum that served to enhance the experience and not diminish it. Asher swung her up in his arms and carried her into his bedroom, where an enormous, ornate wood and iron bed dominated the room.

They tore at each other's clothes, anxious to get the skin on skin contact they so desperately desired. She barely had time to gaze at the gorgeous man who seemed to want her as much as she wanted him—that is, if the size and hardness of his cock was any indication. His hands skimmed down her back to her ass to cup it and bring her closer so her stiff nipples grazed his chest.

Nicole managed to get her hand between them and wrapped her fingers around his manhood. Asher thrust his hips forward and back, slowly and gently, hissing as she played with him.

"That's not how this works," he murmured as he tipped her back on the bed.

She braced herself on her elbows and got a good long look at his ripped and muscled body. Just long enough to lock eyes as he sank to his knees and pulled her ass to the edge of the bed. Putting a leg over each of his shoulders, he lowered his mouth to her sex and licked. Nicole's entire body trembled in response.

His tongue swirled around her clitoris before sucking it into his mouth to suckle as one hand slid up her torso to cup and squeeze her breasts before rolling the nipple between his thumb and forefinger and giving it a gentle tug and then a harsher pinch. Nicole gasped, but not in pain. How many times had she wanted some man to give her just a little nip of pain? Nip being the operative word, as he closed his teeth around her clit before laving it with his tongue and then moving down to her core.

Her hips arched up as he speared her with his tongue, diving as deep as he could before flattening it out to lap at her honey. Nicole could barely breathe. She hadn't had that many lovers and none of them—especially Kevin—had ever made her feel even half of this.

She gripped the quilt in her fists and writhed

under his skillful ministrations. Asher was focused on her pleasure as he stroked her clit and feasted on her pussy. He moved from her sheath to her clit, but before she could mourn the loss of his tongue inside her, he penetrated her with two fingers and began to stroke, curling them up to drag along the top of her sheath. He began using his tongue and fingers in tandem to bring her to a quiet, earth-shaking climax —the likes of which she had never even imagined.

Her pussy contracted on his fingers, pulsing in the same way her clit seemed to be doing. Her legs, which were bent over his shoulders, clasped his back, pulling him forward and locking his mouth to her sex. He chuckled against her labia before nipping each one and standing up.

He pulled her back on her feet and then lifted her up, placing her in the bed so she was lying with her head against the headboard and stretched out to the footboard below.

"Do you have any idea how beautiful you are, flushed with that orgasm?"

Nicole was embarrassed and moved her hands to cover herself from the intensity of his gaze.

"No," he growled. "You do not try to hide yourself from me."

He reached down and moved her hands away and then stood, taking her in. She was uncomfortable and she started to bring her hands up again but stopped when he rumbled disapprovingly.

When she obligingly removed her hands, he smiled and crooned, "Good girl."

He crawled onto the bed, covering her body with his own, spreading her legs with his knees as he lowered himself into the space he had made. Asher was the most beautiful man she'd ever seen. He wasn't perfection but the scars made him real. He was every fantasy she'd ever had—sculpted chest, washboard abs, and hung. She had some real concern about whether he'd fit.

Asher fitted his cock to the opening of her core before easing inside her, only to draw back and do it again. Slowly but surely, he pressed a little deeper inside as she clutched at his biceps until finally, he thrust deep and buried himself.

It was the most exquisite pain and she braced herself for him to draw back and do it again. But he didn't, he waited, allowing her body to adjust to his. He gently began to surge in and out, each time searching her face for signs that he was hurting her. Hurt was the wrong word. There was discomfort, but that began to fade in the face of the inordinate pleasure he was inflicting.

Over and over, he pounded into her as her inner walls shook and quivered. She couldn't think; all she could do was feel the intense pleasure he was creating between them. Her breath sped up and the noises she was making were incoherent—somewhere between a moan and a sigh. Her body stiffened in anticipation of what she knew would be a powerful orgasm that would shake her to her core and change everything forever.

Harder and harder he hammered her pussy, until at last he thrust deep and ground himself against her, forcing her into a freefall of ecstasy she had never experienced before. Nicole cried out his name and clung to him, hanging in a place where time and space had ceased to exist. As he nuzzled her neck, he rested on top of her, giving her all his weight but instead of feeling smothered and wanting him to move off, she wrapped her arms around him and held him close, offering him her softness.

Finally, he rolled off her, pulling her close and settling her against his side with her head on his shoulder. His breathing became deep and even, and Nicole lay in the dark next to him, wondering how she knew that everything had changed and nothing would ever be the same again.

NICOLE

What followed was a night of decadent passion and indulgence. Maybe it was because she was technically on vacation, but then again… maybe not. There had been none of the usual awkwardness she felt after having sex with someone. That was probably because Asher made it so clear what his intentions were. He was not looking for a one-night stand. He was looking to start forever.

There were two problems with a happily ever after scenario. One was that she wasn't going to let anything—Asher, eternal love, whatever—get between her and her solo climb in the morning. This climb was important to her on so many different levels, most of which she probably couldn't articulate. The other was that she wasn't sure she wanted forever with anybody, let alone a park ranger in the middle of Nowhere, Alaska. The pull to acquiesce and to fall into a hedonistic sexual relationship was strong, but Nicole had learned that if she didn't put her needs and desires first, neither would anyone else.

Sleep had been elusive, but finally it had come. When she opened her eyes, she did so slowly so that if he was awake, he wouldn't necessarily know she was. She could hear his deep and even breathing beside her. When she'd finally managed to roll away from him so she could sleep, Asher had rolled behind her, spooning his body to hers and resting his arm around her waist. Instead of feeling trapped, she'd felt safe and secure.

She glanced at the mantel clock sitting on top of his tallboy dresser. Shit! It was after four. She'd hoped to be away from here long before now. The fact was her original plan had not included spending the night, not to mention having sex with a hunky park ranger. She didn't imagine he slept much past six. Nicole reasoned that if she hurried, she'd be able to make it back to her hotel room, grab a quick shower and dress. Her climbing gear was already packed. She had protein bars with her for later but would grab a Diet Coke and something from McDonald's to eat en route to Pyramid Mountain.

Today was the day, and she needed to get going. Her spirit wanted to get to the mountain and prove to herself that she could do it. Her mind wanted to stay in bed with Asher and revel in the way he made her feel. Her body, however, thought her mind and spirit were nuts. It was all she could do not to groan as she slipped from under his arm and swung her legs off the bed.

When she glanced at him, she could see he was deeply asleep. She sat up, waited, and held her breath, to see if her movement had awakened him or if she could slip away quietly to complete her mission. That's what it felt like—a mission to prove she could set out to do what she wanted. She done that professionally and was closing in on the time Judith would make her a partner. But this trip, this solo technical climb, had taken on a meaning of its own. She wasn't sure she could explain it to anyone.

As she stood up, she barely managed not to sink to her knees to grumble about the size of his dick and how many times he'd made her come. It felt like he'd knocked something loose inside, but damn… at the time it had been amazing. Her muscles were stiff, sore, and didn't want to cooperate. Nicole wasn't convinced that hadn't been part of his goal.

Nicole moved silently throughout the room and the rest of his cabin. She managed to slip on just enough clothes to be presentable if anyone saw her going into her hotel room. At the front door to his cabin, she glanced back at the bedroom door. Hopefully, he would understand her need to do this alone. She knew she was taking the coward's way out, but also knew if she woke him, he'd talk her out of it.

She climbed into her cold, rented SUV and

headed back to the hotel. Now that she was away from his cabin, speed and not stealth was her goal. She managed to park close to her hotel room and got herself inside without anyone seeing her. She made short work of showering, dressing, and loading her things into the back of the SUV. She pulled out of the hotel's parking lot in a little less than half an hour, stopped at McDonald's to get a breakfast sandwich and a Diet Coke, thankful they were open twenty-four hours a day. From the driveway of the fast-food restaurant, she headed out of town to Pyramid Mountain.

Instead of the parking lot for the trailhead, which had yet to open, she opted to find a place she could pull completely off the road. She wrote a note, leaving it on the dash, which would let anyone know where she was headed and her estimated time of arrival back at her vehicle. She got into her climbing gear and made sure her pack was ready to go.

Taking a deep breath, she let it out and began the hike to the base of the mountain. It wasn't difficult terrain at first and she could allow her mind to wander and consider things other than like where to put her feet. She thought back to the night before.

She could easily remember his lips against hers, the feel of him as he settled between her legs before thrusting up into her. His hands skimming over her skin, reaching beneath her to hold her steady and the deep, resonant purring that seemed to emanate from his chest.

Over and over, he'd taken her to heights of ecstasy she'd never even known she could achieve. Her body had learned to yield to his and let him lead her to a level of intimacy and desire she'd never known before. He'd been almost insatiable, but then so had she. She couldn't ever remember wanting a man the way she'd wanted him.

Nicole was fairly certain he was going to be angry, but she'd never once said she wasn't going to make her solo climb. She hoped they'd be able to talk it through and he'd still want her to stay at least through the weekend. The problem was, he wanted more, and she wasn't sure she was ready to give that to him or to anyone else.

She started up from the base of the mountain. The trail was a little over two and a half miles. As Asher had said, the first third wasn't too bad, although she did have to do some scrambling to make much headway. The next third was a mixture of scrambling and mountain climbing. Her new crampons came in handy when she hit the ice and the snow seemed to go from ankle to waist deep in less than fifty yards.

Using her snow poles, she continued up, stopping to catch her breath. She'd really believed she was in shape, but although Pyramid Mountain wasn't a particularly high peak, the last third was most definitely a technical climb and her new ice axe and ice tool came in handy as she began rigging her lines to make it to the summit.

The beautiful blue skies of the morning gave way to gray storm clouds and the sun began to play behind them before disappearing altogether. Nicole was making her way up from the bottom of the top third of the mountain, determined to reach the summit. She began using her new equipment to pierce the snow and ice and set her anchors for her pitons, roping herself in as she went.

Nicole was all too aware that climbing was inherently risky, solo technical climbs even more so. What had looked like an easy climb to claim as her first solo was rapidly becoming far more dangerous than she'd expected. Simple errors could have, she knew, tragic and deadly consequences. But as far as she was concerned, there was no turning back.

Using both the ice axe and ice tool in conjunction with her crampons, she made her way slowly up the icy face of the mountain. Snow was beginning to fall and adding a degree of difficulty she hadn't anticipated. She admitted, only to herself and only for a moment, that it might have been better to heed Asher's advice and not tried to make the climb today. But dammit, this was when she'd planned to do it.

Over and over, she swung her ice equipment and crampons into the ice, making her way slowly but surely to the top. Finally, she was able to stand on top of Pyramid Mountain, anchored by her beautiful ice axe and ice tool, and gloried in her achievement. A strong gust of arctic wind tried to topple her from the top and wrest her victory away from her, but Nicole stood strong. Then she began her slow descent down the mountain.

She might try to rappel once she got lower but didn't feel confident enough in her skills to do so over the glacial terrain. For a small mountain, she could now see why Asher had urged caution. She made her way carefully down, moving her pitons and testing each one before looping herself in and belaying her way down.

Nicole was making good progress, when she pulled down to check the strength of one of her anchors and it popped out. She was surprised as a gust of wind caught her like a rag doll and blew her away from the anchor that had been attached to the mountain. She reached out with the ice axe, trying to self-arrest and regain control of her body and her descent.

She had almost pulled herself back into position when her climbing cord snapped and she began to plummet down the side of the mountain. Nicole had practiced enough falls that she was able to free her ice axe and tool and slam both into the sheer sheet of ice covering the mountain's face. She came to a hard and abrupt halt on a wide, rocky ledge.

Shit!

If she'd thought her sexual marathon with Asher the night before had made her a little sore, it was nothing compared to this. She lay perfectly still for a moment as the sky above her became white and the snow began falling in earnest. She assessed her body for injuries. Her left wrist was sore, but from what she could feel with her gloved hand, it didn't seem broken. Nor did anything else.

She eased her way into a sitting position and looked at the cord, hoping she had just forgotten to tie it off properly, but she could see it had snapped. That didn't seem right, as she'd bought new ropes for her solo ascent. She still had one rope, but with a bad wrist, aching ribs, and only one rope, it was likely beyond her ability to save herself.

Nicole rolled her eyes. She had just become one more statistic for Asher to quote when cautioning people to not underestimate Pyramid Mountain. If she was going to fall, though, at least she had done so after she made the summit.

She looked up at the sky and *tsk tsked* herself as it appeared the storm was gaining intensity. She thought about trying to suck it up and make it down on her own, but every breath hurt. She didn't think she'd broken a rib or punctured a lung, but she didn't fancy trying to get off the mountain without aid. She hated putting anyone else at risk, but with the weather closing in, all delaying would do was put her rescuers in greater danger.

Reaching into her pack, Nicole found the emergency beacon and turned it on. There was something reassuring about its steady bleep-bleep-bleep and flashing red light. She sat it up on her tripod to keep it out of the snow. She was quite certain if she and Ash got together again, he would take her to task for sneaking out of his cabin and making her solo climb.

Nicole was fairly sure Asher would be the one to come to her aid and she was equally sure she would hear that sexy baritone voice of his admonishing her for her recklessness and foolishness. But he was wrong, she had been neither. She might not have been as cautious as he might have liked but except for the falling down the mountain and needing to be rescued, her first solo climb had been a success.

Pulling her thermal, water-resistant blanket from her pack, she managed to get it underneath and wrapped around her to ward off hypothermia. She might have been more worried, but she knew the ranger station was near and knew Ash would most likely be on his way already. Regardless of what might or might not happen in the future, she owed the sexy ranger her thanks and a bottle of really good whiskey.

As darkness began to close in, Nicole waited and pulled the blanket over her head. She wasn't waiting for her knight in shining armor, but rather for a pissed off ranger with dark eyes and a killer body.

CHAPTER 9

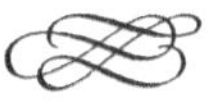

ASHER

When Asher woke, the sun had already cleared the eastern horizon. He could feel the lack of her presence and swore under his breath. He had actually believed he'd talked her out of trying to make her solo climb.

He couldn't remember the last time he'd used a woman as hard and as thoroughly as he had his mate the night before. Nor could he recall waking this late in the day. She didn't know she was his fated mate, but that really wasn't the point. The fact of the matter was, she probably had no knowledge that the fantastical creatures her favorite romance writer wrote about were in fact real.

Asher kept his eyes shut as he reached down and stroked the massive erection he'd awakened with and had planned to ease within her soft, wet heat. Never had any female—shifter or human—felt like she did.

It was as if she had been created just for him. She'd been snug, but she had writhed beneath him, easily climaxing when he wanted her to.

He wanted to ignore his state of arousal but knew it would be easier and quicker to take care of it himself so made a fist around his cock and began to stroke, remembering the way her pussy had clamped down on him time and time again as he pounded into her, crying out as she came, and he filled her with his seed. As he fisted himself faster and harder, he recalled how her velvet sheath felt wrapped around his dick. Groaning, Asher came, making a mess of the bed as his release puddled on the sheets.

As they had made dinner and talked about the difficulties Pyramid Mountain presented this time of year to even the most skilled climber, much less a novice, he had begun to believe he was making progress and that he'd be able to dissuade her from her folly. He'd obviously been wrong. She had lulled him into thinking she would give up the idea of a solo climb and they'd go together.

She'd also made him believe she would stay at least for the weekend. He was arrogant enough to think if he could keep her in his bed for the next four or five days, he could persuade her to give up both her humanity and her life in Seattle and become one with him. Was he wrong about that too?

Asher crawled out of bed, stripping the sheets and tossing them into the combo washer/dryer that he'd installed in his walk-in closet. Before hitting the start button, he headed into the bath, noting she hadn't used it before leaving. Smart. If she'd turned on the shower, the sound would have awakened him and he would have joined her, giving her a better way to while away the hours before he had to be at work, leaving her here to relax and make herself at home.

He dried himself, tossing the towel in with the sheets and then got dressed. He really hoped she was enjoying herself, because she was very likely in for her first taste of discipline when he caught up with her. He'd have breakfast, head into the office, and unless there was something more pressing to do, he'd head out to search for her rental vehicle.

Before leaving his cabin, he turned on the washer/dryer unit and made his way out to the kitchen to make something to eat. His cooking repertoire was meager at best, but he could make a decent scramble or omelet. He diced up cooked ham, peppers, and onions. He shredded pepper jack cheese and cracked open three eggs, whisking them together before pouring them into his omelet pan. He hadn't lied to her about not being a great cook, but he could make a pretty good omelet or egg scramble and get himself fed if he needed to.

He put a pod of dark roast coffee in his coffeemaker and by the time it was brewed, his omelet was finished. A little salt and pepper over the top and he sat down at his counter to eat. He held the coffee mug up under his nose and inhaled deeply. There was little in this world that could compare to the smell of a good cup of coffee. He grinned. One of the few things that could was the smell of Nicole's arousal. It was almost as sweet as her taste.

Asher was just about to lift it to his lips to take a sip when the phone rang. He glanced at the caller ID —damn, it was Randy.

"Randy, it had better be important, my food is getting cold."

"The storm is worse than predicted. The snow is bad, but there's an arctic wind driving it and we're getting reports of storm surge all along the coast."

"Has the beacon we gave Nicole gone off?"

"No. Isn't she with you?"

"Unfortunately, not. I'll need to head up to Pyramid, but I'll head into the office first."

"Good. I'll see you when you get here."

Asher finished his food, grabbed his gear and headed out to his vehicle. Randy hadn't been exaggerating, the snow was blowing almost sideways. He looked at the sky; there was no sign of it letting up. He used the ice scraper and sweeper he kept in his SUV to clear his front and back windshields as well as the windows. Once inside, he let the vehicle warm up before putting it in gear and heading towards the Kodiak Island ranger station.

He couldn't believe Nicole had managed to get up and get away without waking him nor that he had slept so late. He grinned. He supposed he could chalk up the latter to being sated and snuggled up to his fated mate.

Listening to the radio reports in his SUV, he surmised that Nicole had probably gotten to the mountain *before* the snow had really begun to fall in earnest. But he had to admit the road crews in and around the city of Kodiak did an excellent job at getting them clear and relatively safe to drive. Granted most everyone on the island was prepared and experienced with driving in extreme weather, but still the crews that were out and about made it a whole lot easier for people to get to and from wherever they needed to go.

He stopped twice to help people who had pushed their luck and skill just a bit far and ended up in a ditch. By the time he reached the office, the sun had gone past the mid-day point in the sky. It was difficult to tell because all he could see of the sun was a yellow glow behind the clouds that kept dumping snow all over the island.

Asher parked and headed inside the station. "Any casualties we need to deal with?"

"Not so far, but that emergency beacon you gave Nicole just went off. I matched the geo coordinates to the tracking map, and it seems she's somewhere in the mid-range of the mountain. When I looked at the tracking history, it hasn't moved in the past half hour. The storm is far worse than they predicted.

It's rolling in with snow, sleet, and lots of cold wind."

"Damn it," growled Asher. "Let's get HQ on the line and let them know we have a search and rescue in progress. Give the paramedics a heads up. Coordinate her position with the fastest way down."

"Do you want me to go with you?" asked Randy.

"No. I need you to coordinate things from the office. I'll find her and make an assessment. If I don't think I can get her off the mountain by myself, we'll get one of the volunteers to come in and man the office until you can get to us. I'm taking another beacon as well as the emergency aid kit and gear to get her warm and off the mountain."

"I hoped you'd talked her out of doing this climb."

"I thought I had. Guess I was wrong. I'll make sure she thinks long and hard about challenging the Alaskan wilderness by herself again."

"Stay safe, boss."

"You, too."

Asher checked the weather report again. Knowing his body would need fuel, he grabbed a couple of protein bars, made a pot of coffee and filled two big thermoses, then grabbed some emergency heat packs. In most rescues, the most serious threat was hypothermia. He dumped some of the remaining hot coffee in his travel mug and headed out the door.

He knew time was of the essence. If Nicole had

activated the beacon, she was in trouble. She was too stubborn and too proud to have done so if she'd had any other choice. He'd made a few passing references to spanking a disobedient mate the day before and instead of being appalled, her pupils had dilated in arousal. He knew there were some wolf-shifters who still believed in corporal punishment to keep their she-wolves in line, but Asher saw it more as a way for him to express his dominance in a way that might make her think twice about doing something a second time, but also ramp up her arousal.

Asher drove to the trailhead and her SUV was not in the parking area. Most likely it hadn't been opened when she'd arrived. He had to give her credit for being able to sneak out of the cabin, as well as knowing him well enough to know that as soon as he found her gone, he'd come looking for her.

He was looking for where she'd stashed her car when his sat phone rang. It was Randy.

"Randy? Has the beacon moved?"

"No, and boss, we've got big trouble."

Shit! That wasn't good.

"Bigger than a novice climber who is likely injured on the side of a mountain?"

"Yeah. The storm hit that research group's base camp. They've been trapped by flooding and storm surge. They have two injured—one critically from when one of the beams fell on him and the other, they think, is having a heart attack. I've called in for back-up, but HQ is saying all of our resources need to be devoted to getting those government researchers out of there."

Asher growled. "HQ can shove it. If the winds are that bad, Nicole will freeze to death. The chopper isn't viable. Get hold of as many volunteers as you can. Leave two of them at the office to coordinate and take the rest on snowmobiles to get the scientists out. Turn loose any animal that can be and euthanize those that can't. The scientists are not going to like losing their data, but I don't give a damn. Let them know they need to be prepared to leave as soon as you get there. Take an emergency aid kit with you as well as emergency heat packs. If their structure is compromised, most likely they don't have heat."

"I've already put out the call to our volunteers and they're coming in. Joe is closing up shop and bringing extra supplies. But HQ said they wanted you to coordinate from on site."

"My territory; my call. You and the volunteers are closer, and we already know Nicole's in trouble. If HQ doesn't like it, they can fire my ass."

"Got it. We won't let you down, boss."

"I'll have the sat phone with me, so if you need me, just call. I have every confidence in you and our volunteers."

Ash ended the call, irrationally angrier at Nicole than he'd been before. It wasn't her fault the storm was causing more trouble than anticipated, and he bet the researchers hadn't enacted any of the safety and back-up protocols they'd laid out for them two months ago. He wondered why it was that people simply disregarded the advice of people trained to know better than them. It made no sense at all.

He made his way out of the trailhead parking lot, stopping long enough to put the gate in place, locking it off. If people were on the road, they were better off limping into the city or seeking shelter at someone's house along the road. Parking in the lot was a bad idea as it would be easy to get snowbound inside your vehicle and freeze to death. Most Alaskan residents carried emergency supplies and knew how to handle unexpected, severe storms like the one headed in.

As he searched for Nicole's rented SUV, he called Jax up in Mystic River to make sure he had everything buttoned down up there.

"Asher?" he answered.

"The one and only. Just wanted to call and make sure the storm didn't catch you by surprise."

"No. We've been watching the weather service. I heard that group of researchers managed to get themselves into trouble."

"Not a big surprise. I sent Randy and a bunch of our volunteers up there to get them out. I have two more at the office."

"Where are you?"

"I'm headed up Pyramid Mountain to get a

novice climber who thought it was the perfect day and peak to make her first solo ascent."

"They never learn. They look at that cute little mountain and think anyone can do it, but they are dead ass wrong. Do any of them even bother to read the degree of difficulty ratings assigned to that mountain? You think you'll get to her in time?"

"I'd better."

"Any particular reason?"

"She's my fated mate."

"Your what?"

"You heard me. Don't make me say it again. Actually, I think that's the first time I've said it out loud."

"Damn."

Asher chuckled. "I know. And better yet? She's human."

He'd known that would give Jax a good laugh. "Have fun with that."

"I will. She likes Maddie Owen's books so I'm hoping she'll have less difficulty accepting that shifters exist and that she is the fated mate to one."

"Only you, Ash; only you. Go get your girl. I'll double check on everyone at Wolf Run. Be safe."

"Will do. You, too."

He ended the call and continued driving until he saw where Nicole had parked her car. He sent the coordinates of his and her vehicles and then got out and put together a rescue kit, including two snow poles and a stretcher he could rig to be a travois in case she was unable to travel under her own steam. He packed additional blankets, the emergency heat packs, and as much of the first aid kit as he'd be able to use on the side of the mountain.

The snow had grown thick, and the arctic wind was howling out of the north. There was absolutely no one around, Asher raised his face to the sky and answered the lonely wind's call with one of his own. Pulling his ski cap into place, he secured his hood over that with his goggles so he could see through the glare. Checking his geo coordinator, he began to track the emergency beacon.

Once he had his gear packed and ready to go, he put his head down and began the long, arduous climb to get to Nicole. He only hoped her injuries weren't life threatening and that she knew enough to protect herself for several hours from the mind-numbing cold as the temperature dropped to lethal levels.

CHAPTER 10

*C*old.

It was damn cold. She had thought when she moved from San Francisco to Seattle it was cold, but no… this was a hell of a lot colder. At this point she knew she wasn't bordering on freezing, but she was cold. She wanted to be back at Asher's… back in that lovely shower she'd used last night and then in his bed. At this point, she was cold enough that she'd settle for that crappy shower in the hotel, but she really wanted to be sharing Asher's body heat.

Nicole was trying to keep her mind active with remembering how long it had been since she'd fallen and had to resort to turning on the emergency beacon. She wondered if having to be rescued off the side of the mountain *after* summiting meant she could claim this climb as her first solo climb. Maybe she could call it her first attempt, although it might be more impressive if her first attempt had been something more impressive like Denali.

Cold. She tried to remember how long in these circumstances she could wait to be rescued before she needed to be concerned about hypothermia. She didn't feel as cold as she had before, and she was getting sleepy. No. That wasn't good. She was pretty sure both of those led to hypothermia. The good news was her wrist didn't hurt as much. It was still difficult to draw a deep breath without pain, but she was certain Asher was coming. How she knew, she wasn't sure, but she could feel it. Asher was coming.

Asher. There was a real puzzle. Nicole really wasn't a one-night stand kind of girl, regardless of how sexy the man in question was. What was bothering her was she wasn't at all sure she wanted it to be a one-night stand. Sure, the sex had been good. Who was she kidding? The sex had been off-the-charts amazing. But there had been something more… hadn't there? At least for her.

She'd been drawn to Asher from the first moment she laid eyes on him. Nicole hoped she'd been able to mask that, but she wasn't sure if he'd ripped her clothes off and thrown her on the desk in his office to have at her that she would have put up more than a token protest. She gave a little laugh. The protest wouldn't be of his treatment of her; it would be that Randy had been there. If they'd been alone and he'd made a move, she'd have been all in. What was a bit disconcerting was she wasn't all that sure she would have tried to stop him even if they'd had a room full of people.

He was going to be pissed. No doubt about that. She hadn't exactly lied to him. Never once had she said she was or wasn't going to make her solo climb. Granted, she'd let him believe she had given it up. She hadn't wanted to argue, and besides, she'd been far more interested in kissing Asher and getting him naked than she had in convincing him she was right. After all, when she'd successfully made her climb, she'd have proven her point. Only now here she was, trying to keep from freezing to death, listening to that annoying beacon and waiting for what she was sure was going to be an unpleasant confrontation with her new lover.

New lover? First off, it wasn't like she had a lot of old lovers, but was that what she was really thinking? What was Asher thinking? He'd said a lot of things last night that made her think he was thinking of a future with her in it. Had he just said what he thought she wanted to hear in order to get her in his bed? Maybe she was going through all these mental gymnastics for nothing. Maybe it was just a case of he was horny, and she was some out-of-town tourist and was available.

But, no, she didn't believe that.

What would a relationship with Asher look like, though? She lived in Seattle—a great cosmopolitan city—and he lived here on Kodiak. He seemed so much a part of the island. Would he leave it for her? There were plenty of national parks in and around Seattle. It would be far easier for him to relocate than her. And one of them would have to relocate. She couldn't see some kind of long-distance thing where they only saw each other once a month as being viable.

She was an event planner, and while she thought being able to offer Alaska in their repertoire of places to hold a wedding or a corporate retreat was a great addition, she didn't think her soon-to-be partner would want to open a satellite office on Kodiak. The idea of Judith here in Alaska made her smile. Judith's idea of roughing it was anything less than a five-star hotel.

Surely, he wouldn't expect her to give up what would be an incredibly lucrative deal in favor of living here, would he? And yet he seemed to be so much a part of this land. It was far easier for her to imagine herself here than Asher in Seattle. She looked around her; she had to admit the rugged terrain of Alaska rivaled the views from her Gig Harbor home.

Her thoughts drifted back to Asher. That seemed to be happening a lot. As soon as she tried to focus on anything else, her mind went back to him. He was so much like the heroes in the books she liked to read, especially the ones with wolf-shifters. Not werewolves. Not some kind of monster that went through a hideous transformation when turning from man to wolf because of a full moon. She'd never had any interest in being with something like that, even in her darkest fantasies.

But the alpha males Maddie Owen described? Yes, please. Tall, brooding, and able to change from man to beast and back again on a whim. At first her wolf-shifters had just kind of blinked from man into their wolf self, but it had evolved to include a kind of small, magical maelstrom that surrounded them and when it dissipated, the change had occurred.

It was hard to focus. Her mind drifted back to the night before, after they returned from their airboat ride.

Once inside his cabin, they'd gotten naked and down to business. Lying next to him, she felt out of control, and yet peaceful. Even then some part of her had known she was in trouble in terms of figuring out what she wanted.

After a while he'd nudged her and told her he was going to get them something to eat before he had her for dessert. She'd laid there in his bed and watched him pull a pair of sweatpants on. She'd never thought of sweatpants as sexy but watching him having to tuck his rapidly hardening cock into them while giving her a lovely side view of his firm, muscled body and fine ass, she'd changed her mind. Deciding she didn't want to be away from him, she'd hopped out of bed, grabbed his flannel shirt, and pulled it on to cover herself.

She walked into the kitchen of his cabin. Except for the bedroom and attached bath the entire place was one large, open space, dominated by an enormous rock fireplace with a rough-hewn mantle.

"I think I bought the cabin for the fireplace. I liked the location too, but other than the fireplace, it was pretty much a wreck."

"Really? I wish I could see past things. You'd think I would be able to as I can look at an empty space and envision how it would look decorated for an event."

"We're well suited. Look around. This place is functional but that's about it."

"I don't think so at all. It has great bones—the fireplace, the wood floors, the cabinets and counters…"

"All picked out by a friend."

"What kind of friend?" slipped out before she could stop herself.

Asher picked her up, setting her down on the counter. "The kid sister of one of my oldest friends."

"I don't know that I find that reassuring. Big brother's best friend is a hot trend in romance novels these days."

"Do you read a lot of romance novels?"

"There's nothing wrong with that," she said defensively.

"Not at all. Just trying to learn about you, and what makes you tick; what turns you on."

"You," she said, wrapping her arms around his strong neck. "You turn me on."

"Ditto." She snorted and he frowned. "Careful, Nicole. You don't put yourself down or deflect how I feel."

"Is that a rule?" she teased.

He nodded. "Yes, and there will be more of them. You'd best accept that you're going to follow them and when you don't, there'll be consequences."

"What kind of consequences?" She wasn't sure why she was pushing him or what it was she wanted him to say.

"I've found a bit of discipline can do a lot to keep a relationship on the right track."

"What kind of discipline?"

"A firm male hand applied to a shapely feminine backside can go a long way to curbing bad behavior and not allowing things to build up."

Bingo!

She'd never thought of herself as liking any kind of pain and had never been turned on by the idea of some brawny male spanking the heroine, but Maddie Owen's books had changed all that. Now one of her deepest, darkest fantasies was to be put over a lover's knee and have her ass spanked. Well, that and having that same hero thrust his knot up into her.

"Are you threatening to spank me?" she said with a casual laugh.

"No threat. I don't make threats Nicole. I make promises and I want you to know up front what the consequences for things are. So yes, if your behavior is bad enough that it warrants you getting your backside blistered, I'm the man to get the job done."

There had been a moment where his comment just hung in the air between them, but then he seemed to back down. "Be a good girl, and I won't have to resort to that."

She couldn't say why, or at least admit it to herself, but there had been a part of her that was disappointed.

He stroked her cheek with his finger. "What's the matter, Nicole? Did you want me to spank you? If so, all you have to do is ask. I think you'd enjoy a sensual spanking much more than a discipline one. At least, you would if it was done right."

She leaned into him, giving him a view of her full breasts as he looked down at her. "And do you know how do to it right?"

He chuckled. "Absolutely. You insist on doing that solo climb tomorrow and get into trouble, you'd better hope it's bad enough that we have to airlift you to a hospital on the mainland."

"Why?"

"Because if it isn't, you'll get your first taste of a discipline spanking, and all that comes after it."

She hadn't pursued the conversation, not because it didn't intrigue her, but because the idea of the sexy ranger pinning her over his knee, holding her there, and tattooing her ass had an appeal she wasn't ready to deal with. Something about the way he calmly informed her she would answer to him had inflamed the simmering arousal she had just from being with him.

Now, sitting on the side of the mountain, probably freezing to death, she wondered if he got here in time and she wasn't too far gone if he'd wait to get her home—when had she begun to think of Alaska as home?—to spank her, or if maybe he would do it right here? She shook her head. Now she was really going off the deep end.

Cold.

She was so cold. And sleepy. She was sleepy too. She really hoped Asher got here before she died. She'd like to see him again.

CHAPTER 11

ASHER

The hike to get from the Jeep to the base of the mountain had gone fairly easily. But once he'd started up the slope, he could tell it was going to be hard going. Asher checked his geo tracker. The beacon was still working, and he was on the right trail to get to her.

The sat phone rang. "Randy?"

"HQ says you're to abort the attempt to get to the lone hiker and help get the researchers out."

"I don't much give a damn. Do you feel you can't lead the rescue to the base camp? Or that you don't have the right people?"

"No, but…"

"No buts. As I said, my territory; my call. Tell them I refused."

"I wouldn't do that to you, Ash."

"You may not have a choice. If someone wants to

make a deal, and they will if any of those city slicker researchers gets hurt, they'll check the sat phone logs. So, get up there and get those idiots. I'm not letting Nicole die on Pyramid Mountain because the brass doesn't want an incident where federal employees get hurt."

"They won't get hurt on my watch. Go get your girl."

"I didn't say she was my girl."

"No, you didn't, but it's all over town that the two of you had lunch and then spent the rest of the day together. Don't get me wrong; I know you'd be going, regardless, but it's just nice to see you interested in a girl. She seemed nice. A handful, but nice."

"Ain't nothing wrong with a handful so long as you know how to handle it," quipped Ash with a smile. "If HQ calls again, ignore them. If they have an issue, I'll deal with it. I'll tell them those were my orders, and we were too busy trying to save people's lives to continue to answer their phone calls."

Randy chuckled. "You really have no use for the brass, do you?"

"Not much. I get it, though, they have to take the irate phone calls from the senators, who took them from the companies and families involved, but they don't have their own boots on the ground. You either trust the people who do or get different people. Anything else can get people killed. Trust me on that."

"I do. If it comes to it, I'll choose your orders over anyone else's. Be careful— the news we're getting on the storm isn't good."

"I'll get Nicole and get her down off the mountain. If she activated the emergency beacon, she's hurt or in trouble. I'll need to assess her situation and condition, get her safe, and then I'll head into the office if I can. Stay in touch."

The snow was falling faster and wasn't melting. It was mixed with ice pellets and the two were freezing into a crunchy kind of ground cover that was only going to get worse as the storm raged on. The arctic wind that was screaming down from the north was going to make everything just that much more treacherous.

Asher slogged through the snow and ice, using his poles to propel him forward. This was not going to be an easy trip, but as he began the ascent, he realized the way up to her might possibly be a lot rougher than he'd first thought and could be almost impossible to come back down. He knew the mountain had no caves or even overhangs to speak of. No, they would need to get off the mountain in order to find shelter from the storm.

Oftentimes, knowing what you needed to do and actually doing it were two completely different things. He looked up the incline into blinding white. He could see little beyond about six feet in front of him. Even if he could get to her in time, there was a very real possibility one or both of them would die on the way down.

There was nothing to do but build a travois, remove his clothes and shift. As a wolf, he could haul his things and what he needed to get to her and make much better time. The problem was there was little cover for him to change back without her seeing him. He couldn't think about all the consequences of her seeing him shift. That would have to come later. Perhaps she could be persuaded to keep his secret. If not, they could chalk it up to delusions induced by her trauma. In any event, he had no choice.

He readied the travois, packing his things away. The last things he removed were his boots. Once they and all the other supplies were packed away, he called forth his great wolf. The beast had been prowling around in his psyche, waiting to be let free. The swirling mist mixed with the snow and ice that was blowing faster and faster. The electrical charge of the shift sizzled when it made contact with the ice. The shards of color seemed to crackle and fracture from contact with the frozen air.

Shifting in these conditions was not ideal, but if he had any chance at saving Nicole he needed to do so. The shift seemed to take longer than usual, and at one point he thought it would fail. But his wolf was a fierce predator, and his mate was at risk. He would not be denied.

Finally, he felt his body shift and morph into that

of his altered self. He'd engineered the harness so he could slip into it and then began to move steadily and at a quicker pace than before. The trail was still treacherous, but Asher knew he'd never have been able to conquer the incline and the weather as a human.

He'd rigged the geo tracker to the end of one of the poles on his travois and checked to make sure he was still on the right path. He was a little off, so he reassessed the best way to get to her and started again.

Hang on, baby, I'm coming. He pushed into the harness and pulled with all his strength as he increased his speed from a walk to a trot. He had to get there.

Asher moved, making as much headway as he could. The geo tracker started to beep like a Geiger counter. It wouldn't start until he was within one hundred yards of his goal and would increase in speed as he grew closer. The rapidity of the beeps was reassuring, as they came closer and closer together.

When a particularly hard gust of wind knocked him sideways, it took him life threatening moments to get back on track. He was close enough now that the beeping combined with the buzzing in his brain meant he could feel her presence. He could also feel that her life force was slipping away.

He could feel the change in terrain through the pads of his paws and could now detect her scent. He was almost there. Now he could see an abnormal lump in the snow. It wasn't a good sign that it had covered her. It meant she was most likely unconscious.

Asher began to paw at the snow covering her body like a frozen shroud and laid his muzzle against her throat, feeling for a pulse. It was there, but it was slow and thready. Nicole was dying, and she didn't have long to live. She'd never make it down the mountain. He grabbed her jacket at the shoulder and pulled her out of the snow.

He made sure she wouldn't fall off the ledge that she'd managed to reach in her fall. Her ice axe and ice tool were wedged into the ice. She'd managed to self-arrest her fall and had most likely saved her own life. It took a steady nerve and good training to pull off a maneuver like that. He'd be sure to praise her for that… right after he blistered her backside for her foolishness.

He needed to be human. There was no way he could get her out of her wet clothes, wrap her in blankets and use the emergency heat packs to start to rewarm her. Without knowing her core temperature, it wasn't possible to tell if she was too far gone. It didn't matter, though. He would not give up on her. He would not lose his fated mate before they had even had a chance to really begin.

He unlatched the flap of the pack, leaving the clothes inside to stay as dry as possible. Bracing himself for the cold, he made his wolf relinquish control and pulled on his clothing as quickly as possible. Once he could function, he prepared the travois, layering hypothermic blankets and stripping her out of her wet things, flinging them as far away from her as possible.

Asher lifted her onto the travois, folding the blankets around her so the softest one was next to her skin and the mylar surface of the outer blanket was on top, protecting her from the wet. He pulled a knit ski cap over her head and then tucked her into the blankets so only her eyes would show. The first aid kit was useless at this point and so he discarded it, also.

He would need as light a load as possible to make it down the mountain with as much speed as they needed. When it was safe to do so, he'd return to pick up their things. His plan was to remove his remaining clothes, which were getting soaked and leave them and the satchel behind. Asher activated the emergency heat packs, placing them under her arms, between her thighs, snugged against the bottom of her feet and on top of them, as well as along her neck and all over her torso.

He was tucking her back in as he felt her life beginning to slip away.

"No! No! No! You do not get to die on me," he roared.

He looked to the sky.

"You can't have her. I swear if she lives, I won't discipline her for this stupid stunt," he bargained with the powers that be.

He put his ear to her chest, her heart was still beating, but it, like her breathing was slowing and drawing to an end. Asher knew that what he was about to do went against everything he believed in. He'd had little respect for male wolves who turned their human mates without said human's consent. It was not something to be done lightly or capriciously. The woman would be giving up her humanity.

Too many times, especially if the woman didn't want it or was too weak, the transition could kill her. The dilemma he now faced was that she was about to die. She was unconscious. Even if he was willing to allow her to say no, she was unconscious and unable to give her consent—freely or otherwise.

Nicole was dying. He had one chance and one chance only to save her. He moved the emergency heat pack from the side of her neck. Leaning down, he kissed the spot between the hollow of her throat and the beginning of her clavicle. Nicole was too weak to struggle but she moaned. If this worked, he would have a lot of explaining to do. If not, she would be dead, and he would face a long and lonely life without her until he could join her on the other side. Or, if the poets and bards were to be believed, by claiming his mate, he linked his life inextricably to hers and would follow her into the great beyond within a year. It seemed like the best deal he could make with the devil.

He kissed the spot again, willing his canines to

lengthen and sharpen into fangs capable of ripping and tearing flesh. He growled possessively and sank his teeth into her neck, feeling and tasting her blood as it flowed into his mouth. The bite was savage and created a great gaping wound for his DNA to invade her body, overwriting it and making her one with him.

Nicole was too weak to even react, and he doubted she even felt the pain he'd inflicted with the brutal bite. He released her neck, kissing the wound and reached for the discarded first aid kit, removing the bandaging he'd need to protect the wound. Perhaps she was so far gone it wouldn't work. Perhaps she would never awaken again to know what he'd done. Or perhaps she would go through the transition and come out the other side, never becoming aware of the change her body had gone through.

Whatever happened, it was obvious to him that if he was to give her the best shot at survival, he needed to head north to Mystic River and to Wolf Run. If she had any hope of survival it would be with a pack that had seen more than its fair share of transitioning she-wolves—his own mother included.

Asher finished the bandaging, replaced the heat pack, and tucked her back into the blankets. After using her new goggles to shield her eyes and secure the blankets around her head, he lashed her ice axe and ice tool on either side of the travois to give it more strength and stability and hopefully to keep her from falling off.

This time instead of removing his clothing he just called forth his wolf. The clothing would never survive, but he would be warmer and safer as a wolf. Besides, he always kept a set of winter weather clothing in his Jeep. Once more the controlled chaos of the shift surrounded him, whirling in eddies of electricity, color, and light and interacting with the gathering intensity of the storm. When he was once more wolf, he maneuvered back into the harness, leaned in, and began the perilous journey back down the mountainside.

Most people would have thought going down the treacherous slope would be easier and safer than going up, but Asher knew it wasn't. The weight of the travois with Nicole on board pushed at him from behind as he slipped and slid his way down. Again, wolf paws were better for this sort of thing than human feet, even with crampons on.

He breathed a sigh of relief when at long last he could see his Jeep. It was being buried by the storm, but he would be able to get it out. When he reached the back of the Jeep, he opened the hatch, shifted, and crawled in to swiftly pull on his clothes and spare snow boots. He laid down the back seat and layered the dry blankets he kept in there and propped a pillow up behind the passenger seat. That way he could reach her if he had to.

Asher looked at Nicole as she lay on the travois and prepared to move her into the vehicle and rewrap her in completely dry blankets and new heat packs, leaving those he had discarded in a small pile wedged between the rocks. He listened to her heart and breathing as he took her pulse. It might only be wishful thinking, but everything seemed to be improving.

Once he had her secure, he started the Jeep to let it warm up before heading North. He called Randy on the sat phone.

"Boss? What a clusterfuck. These people might be smart about whatever it is they're doing, but they haven't got one grain of common sense between them."

Asher smiled. "Did we lose any of the animals they've been studying?"

"No, we didn't. That, at least, they did right. We've got them secured and are heading back to Kodiak. Did you get to Nicole in time?"

"I think so. She's touch and go. I'm heading up to Mystic River."

"Why not Kodiak or get her to the mainland?"

"My father has his own medical facility. I can be assured she'll get the best care there. Besides there's no way to get to the mainland with this storm. I'm going to drive as far as I can and have a friend meet me with a couple of snowmobiles. I'll let you know when I get her to Mystic River. You let me know when you've got them safely back to town. Any injuries?"

"No. They were able to airlift the two guys they needed to, and the rest are just a little bumped and frazzled. They'll be fine. HQ is none too happy with you, though."

"Fuck HQ. We got everybody saved, including, I hope, Nicole. Stay in touch."

"You, too. And Boss?"

"Yeah, Randy."

"I hope she pulls through."

"You and me both. I have a good feeling about it. She's tough and strong."

As he ended the call, he looked back on Nicole. He prayed he had told Randy the truth and not just shared his wishful thinking. Before pulling out he placed another call—to the sheriff of Mystic River… his friend Jax Miller.

"Jax? I need a favor."

"Name it."

"I need a snowmobile with a covered sled, lined with blankets and heat packs."

"Are you injured?"

"No. My fated mate is suffering from hypothermia. She looks like she's improving but I'm not a doctor."

"I'll have Doc come with me and he can make a cursory examination. But I don't have to remind you how dangerous hypothermia is."

"No, but I'm hoping I turned her in time that the

lycan DNA will kick in and help her fight her way back."

"Why is it I have a sneaky feeling she didn't consent to be turned?"

"What was I supposed to do, let her die? I had no choice."

"Do you want me to let your old man know you're coming home?"

"I haven't made that decision. I'd like to talk to Doc, first."

"Good enough. Where do you want to meet?"

"I'm pretty sure I can get to Maidenhead Point. My guess is about three hours."

"Got it. We'll be there. Let me know if that changes."

Asher ended the call and reached his hand back to touch her. He was smart enough to know her chances weren't good, but he prayed she was the fighter he thought she was.

"Hang on, baby. Fight for me. Fight to live, Nicole. We've got a lot of living and loving to do."

Putting the Jeep in gear, Asher pulled out onto the road, and instead of heading east back to Kodiak, he headed north toward Mystic River, and he hoped, a future with his fated mate.

CHAPTER 12

NICOLE

*N*icole came slowly to consciousness as the warm cocoon in which she'd been resting opened, allowing the killing cold to enter. Strong arms scooped her and the warm, toasty blankets up and strode away, making a crunching sound as he went.

Asher. It was Asher. He was going to be pissed, but for now, she was happy just to have him near.

She could hear and feel a deep rumbling that seemed to call from his spirit to hers. She snuggled against his hard, warm body. Warm was good. It had been so cold on the side of that damn mountain.

Consciousness slipped away again, and she felt herself floating on some plane of existence where time and pain didn't exist. No pain was good. Her brain was slightly fuzzy, but this place was a whole lot better than the cold on Pyramid Mountain.

For the next few days, she was told later, she

hovered between life and death. Death had a certain appeal. It beckoned to her with light and peace, but she didn't want to die. She'd done everything she could to stave off the cold. If she lived, she was pretty sure she owed Asher a debt she could never repay. It would mean he'd gotten to her in time.

She had no actual awareness of her surroundings or what was being done to her, and she couldn't really see or hear anything. Despite this, she knew she was not alone. The rumbling that resonated within her body came from a soothing presence that seemed to be at her side constantly. It never allowed her to do more than turn and look at the light. When she tried to turn and walk toward the light, a dark growling sound forced her to turn back towards it.

The presence—was it Asher?—alternately pleaded and demanded that she remain in the land of the living. She couldn't believe Asher would plead. Demand, yes, but not plead. Whoever he was, he was unwilling to relinquish her to death. Her bemused reverie was disturbed when a blinding agony surged through her system, causing her body to convulse. The deep, calming rumbling increased and strong firm hands stroked her body and bade her to remain, even though she knew death would end her suffering.

Why was he so insistent she endure the torturous pain that seemed to permeate every part of her mind, body and soul? She struggled against the hold he seemed to have over her, but he would not relent. He refused to cede her existence to eternity and beyond.

She wasn't sure it was Asher. Maybe she just wanted it to be. Maybe it was like in the movie *You've Got Mail* when the heroine tells the hero when they meet in the park that she really wanted it to be him all along. It was a silly little movie, but she liked to watch it. It made her feel like serendipity could still provide the perfect soul mate. She knew whoever he was, he was here, and he was providing the tenuous tether she had to this life.

The voice began to speak. It was Asher. "Do not go quietly into eternity. I know it beckons to you. But I need you. You are my fated mate. We are destined to be together. I forbid you to go."

How like him to start out poetically and then just think he could command her to do his bidding. He tended to be a bit high-handed, but he was still the sexiest man she'd ever met, and he did seem to care about her. He was what her romance books called a dominant alpha male. She turned once more to look at the light, but felt strong fingers wrap around her wrist, drawing her back towards the living.

She had to admit, she wanted to live, except for the whole being in a lot of pain and having Asher majorly pissed off at her. Maybe almost dying would make him cut her a little slack. But even though she hadn't known him long, she imagined almost dying would only serve to piss him off more.

Her eyes fluttered open. It was dark, but there was a small amount of ambient light from somewhere behind her.

"Nicole, sweetheart, wake up."

That was definitely Asher's voice, and he didn't sound all that pissed off. "Betty, get Doc. I think she's coming around. Nicole? Can you hear me?"

Part of her wanted just to go back to the warm, fuzzy place where nothing hurt and nobody wanted anything from her, but another part—the greater part—wanted to return to the land of the living and be with Asher.

"Nicole?" said a voice she vaguely remembered but couldn't place for the life of her.

"Nicole, please." She was wrong, Asher could and would plead.

"Come on Nicole; you can do this," said the other male voice.

"Nicole, wake up," commanded Asher.

Now there was the dominant male voice she had come to love. Love? Where the hell did that notion come from? She couldn't be in love with Asher, could she?

"Don't snarl at me," she managed to mumble. "It makes my head hurt, but at least the damn buzzing is gone."

Asher chuckled and kissed her forehead. Fuck that. She grabbed the front of his shirt and pulled him down to where she fused her lips to his. Damn if he didn't take control of the kiss, which was fine by her. She'd never considered herself to be a great kisser, although she did give good blow jobs. Her mind was racing a mile a minute, kind of like an old-style pinball machine—dinging away as it went from pin to pin and she tried to work the controls so the ball stayed in play.

His tongue swept through her mouth, dominating it and enticing hers to come and dance with his in a language that spoke of feelings far deeper than lust. He was in control, his tongue entwining with hers as his hand tangled in her hair, adjusting her head to the position he wanted. The moment she surrendered to him, dominance turned to seduction, coaxing, and tempting her to do the same, but never allowing her to fool herself that she was the one in charge.

"I know it's been a week since you two got to canoodle with each other..."

Asher broke the kiss and both he and Nicole laughed.

She opened her eyes and looked deeply into his— fathomless pools of deep chocolate that she wanted to dive into and wallow in.

"Did he just say canoodle?" she asked.

"I believe he did, but Doc is very old fashioned and genteel," said Asher.

"Not at all like you," she teased.

"Nothing at all. How are you feeling?" he asked.

"If you think you can let your fated mate alone

long enough for me to examine, *I* might be able to answer that for you," said the man Nicole now knew to be Doc.

"He doesn't need a doctor for me to tell him I feel fine," said Nicole.

"I'll be the judge of that, young lady," said Doc.

"Good god, did he just call me 'young lady?'"

"It's a relative term. Compared to him, Methuselah is young," quipped Asher.

"Wolves and their fated mates. I swear, your kind is worse than all of the rest put together," said Doc somewhat jovially.

Wolves? Fated Mates? Didn't Maddie Owen write romance novels about wolf-shifters and their fated mates?

Asher moved from her side to allow Doc to examine her, but he didn't move far—just from one side to the other. Taking her hand in his, he brought it to his lips and kissed it.

"I've missed you," he said to her, his voice soothing.

"How could you miss her?" asked Doc. "You've barely left her side."

"True enough," admitted Asher, "but still, I missed her."

"I missed you too," said Nicole, "but only kind of. I couldn't really see you in my dreams, but I could feel your presence. I knew you were here. For what it's worth, I took comfort in that."

"I'm glad I could help, although I should point

out that had you not slipped out of our bed, I could have been more than a presence and a damn sight more than comforting."

"Where am I?" she asked.

"Mystic River, the town I was born in," answered Asher.

"Born and raised," added Doc. "It's north of both Kodiak and Pyramid Mountain."

"Did I die?" she asked.

"Almost," said Doc. "If it hadn't been for Asher making it up the side of the mountain and giving you emergency aid, getting you warm, and getting you back here, I don't know that you would have made it."

"I don't remember any of that. I remember the fall and I remember my wrist hurting and being cold. I was so cold."

"You had hypothermia. One of the worst cases I've ever seen. Ash got you out of your wet and freezing clothes and into warm, dry, waterproof blankets and then brought you down the side of the mountain in a blizzard. Once there, he changed all of your blankets and had you stretched out in the back of his Jeep. He met Jax—he's our sheriff—with me and a couple of snowmobiles. We changed everything again, got you in a hooded sled and brought you here. You're damned lucky to be alive. My kind doesn't believe much in physical discipline of our mates, but if I ever thought someone deserved it, it's you," Doc scolded.

"Leave her be, old man," growled Asher.

"It's all right babe. I suspect he's telling it like it is to make his point."

"For what it's worth, at one point I made a bargain with whatever power it is that guides our fates, that if you lived, I'd let your reckless foolishness slide this time... but this time only. If you ever do something that foolhardy again, I'll make it so you can't sit down for a week."

She could feel heat suffusing her cheeks. He was blatantly threatening to spank her. It wasn't that he'd made the threat in front of another person that was making her embarrassed, though; it was her reaction to it. Her nipples were puckering, and her pussy was getting ready for him to be thrusting inside her.

The doctor shook his head and completed his examination. "For what it's worth, everything seems to be fine. I want her to take it easy for a few days, but she can be moved up to Wolf Run if you want."

"I don't think that will be necessary. We can either stay at the B and B or I'll ask Jax if we can use his place."

"I hope you mean the house in town. I think she's out of the woods, but I don't want her far from a doctor," said Doc.

Asher nodded. "Wolf Run is further from town than Jax's other place."

"Yes, but your father also has a well-qualified doctor and a state-of-the-art medical facility. You can fault him for a lot of things, but he does take care of his people."

Asher snorted. "Physically."

"Your father lives here?" Nicole asked.

Her own parents were dead. She'd often been glad that they hadn't lived to see how her marriage had ended.

"I'll leave you two alone. I can see you have a lot of explaining to do," said Doc as he left the room.

"So, you're not mad at me?" she asked.

"I was and some part of me still is, but I'm too damn grateful that you're alive to give into my instinct to make sure you never sit comfortably again. I thought we had agreed…"

"I never agreed, but I also deliberately made sure you didn't know that. I probably owe you my life, so thank you for that, and I'm sorry I wasn't as forthright as I might have been."

"Do you understand how close you came to dying?" he asked, not angry but concerned that she didn't fathom the depth of her brush with death.

She nodded. "I think probably closer than you or Doc want me to know."

"I could have lost you before we'd barely begun."

Nicole took her hand in his. "I'm sorry. I only have vague memories about the fall…"

"You fell? I mean I figured because you were propped up on a ledge, but what caused the fall?"

"That's the damndest thing—one of my climbing

cords snapped. If I hadn't bought those two new ice tools… Oh, shit. Do you think there's any chance that we'll be able to find them?"

Asher grinned and pointed to the corner. "I used them as part of the travois to stabilize it and make sure you were secure. I hate to admit it, but you did one hell of a job out there. It took quick thinking and nerves of steel to self-arrest." He kissed her forehead. "Good job."

"Right up to the point I fell off the mountain. I remember my wrist hurting and being so cold. I can sort of recall trying to get myself covered up until you could get to me. I knew you'd come."

"Always, Nicole. I will always come for you. Was your rope in good repair?"

"Yes. Before coming up here I sprang for new top-of-the-line cords. I wanted to make sure nothing could go wrong. I went over them from one end to the other, looking for any defects or fraying. Nothing. They were in perfect shape. I don't understand it," she said, frowning.

"Don't worry about it. We'll take a look when we can get back up there."

"We?" she asked, hopefully.

"We, as in Randy and I or me and one of our volunteers with a lot of experience. I don't want you going up until you're fully healed, and Doc's given you the okay. I need to get up there before then because I left a mess. I was in a hurry to get you down and then up here to Doc."

"Do we need to stay in Mystic River?"

"Until things open back up. At the moment, Mother Nature is playing havoc on the island. We'll probably be here for at least a week."

"Is there a way to communicate with the outside world?"

"Unfortunately," he said, making her laugh. "I'm pretty sure Jax will let us stay at his place here in town. He tends to prefer his home in the mountain. Or if you'd rather, we can see if the B and B has a room. Back when Mystic River was a wild and lawless place, it was a bordello. Now, it's a really pretty place to relax and use as a base for doing things around the town and surrounding wilderness."

The door opened and an arresting man, who could only be Asher's father, entered the room. Nicole felt as if she was looking into the future at what Ash would look like when he was old and had a silver mane of hair. "There's a third and better option. You can come home."

CHAPTER 13

NICOLE

She could see Asher's body take on a posture of tension—his muscles stiffening, his jaw hardening. If he'd been a dog, his hackles would have come up. He stood up, turning to face his father and placing himself—unless she was very mistaken—between the man who had sired him and her. He wasn't frightened or even intimidated. He was wary and angry.

"I think that may be the worst idea you've ever spouted. The last place on earth I'd take Nicole is Wolf Run," Asher said, fighting to keep his tone civil.

Nicole placed her hand on his back, wanting him to know she was with him, and they were together.

"So, that's her name? This woman you brought home?"

"Rest assured, old man. I didn't bring her here to

meet you or even to stay. Hell, I'd have preferred it if she never had to endure your company."

"You watch yourself, boy…"

"Or what? You'll deck me? As I recall, the last time you tried that, I put you on the ground. Try it again, and I just might put you in it."

"Someday, Asher, you and I are going to come to a meeting of the minds."

"Don't bet on it, old man. Now, get out. I don't want you anywhere around Nicole."

The man Asher called father slammed out of the door. Asher prowled around the room, never once moving from between her and the door. What was he thinking? That his father would come back with some goon squad and take them out?

Watching him move with predatory grace, she let thoughts of his father and what trouble might exist between them fade to the back of her mind. Even angry and looking like he hadn't slept in days, he was still gorgeous. She knew for a fact that his sculpted chest tapered to a set of eight-pack abs, sexy hip notches and a ridiculously large cock—a cock he knew how to use to please a woman. Nicole didn't want to think about how many other women there had been. Hundreds? Thousands? No. That was not a path she wanted to go down.

"I take it you and your father don't have the best of relationships?"

"We don't have a relationship at all," he said, sinking down on the mattress beside her.

"Want to talk about it?" she prompted.

He let a bitter chuckle escape his lips. "Am I going to get a choice?"

"I'll let it pass for now. After all you did save my life."

"I did. Don't make me sorry I did that."

"Saved my life?"

"No. Gave you a pass on blistering your ass."

"Would you really?"

"Spank you? Under the right circumstances."

"And what would those be?" she asked provocatively as she walked two fingers up his muscled arm.

This time when he chuckled there was mirth behind it.

"For one thing, if you wanted me to. There are all kinds of spankings, most of which provide for an entirely natural and incredibly aroused response."

"Like a spanking as part of foreplay?"

"Sometimes. But a stress relief spanking, whether it's for the one getting spanked or the one doing the spanking, can also be incredibly erotic. Even a discipline spanking can offer a degree of arousal and need. For the one being spanked, it can allow her to atone for what she's done. For the one administering the discipline, it can allow him to express, in no uncertain terms, his displeasure at the misbehavior. The resultant sex can be powerful and incredibly intimate."

"I imagine the intensity of the spanking varies quite a bit."

"It can. It depends on the couple."

"Would you want to spank me?" she asked, wondering how it was she felt so comfortable talking about sexual spankings to a man she'd only known for a day. Well, apparently more like a week, but she didn't think it counted, as she had been unconscious.

"Truthfully? Yeah. You snuck out…"

"I didn't. I just didn't want to wake you up…"

Asher laughed. "You don't believe that any more than I do. You led me to believe we had an understanding. Then you snuck out of bed. Then you almost died. To say I'm not happy with your behavior is putting it mildly."

"I'm sorry. Is that good enough?"

"It will have to be. I made a deal with whatever powers guide the universe…"

"Would you feel better if you spanked me?" she asked, trying to understand what he was saying and wondering why it was not only arousing, but made sense, both on his part and for her as well.

"Most likely. By surrendering yourself to my authority and trusting me with that gift, I think we'd both feel better—not just me, but you, too. You know you fucked up." She nodded. "I'm not trying to guilt you into anything Nicole. You owe me nothing."

"You saved my life."

"I would have saved anyone up on that mountain.

I save people I don't give a damn about and occasionally even ones I don't like."

"But you have no interest in spanking them…"

"None whatsoever. I don't want a future with them. I don't lo…" he let his voice trail off.

"You don't what?" she asked, holding her breath.

He raked a hand through his hair. "It's too soon for me to say anything. You almost died; you were unconscious. I've had time to process how I feel about you."

"How is that?"

He looked deeply into her eyes. "I love you, Nicole. I want to spend my life with you, and I cannot even fathom a future without you at the center of it."

Nicole had expected an 'I have feelings for you,' statement, or him asking her to stay the weekend…

"Wait, what day is it?" she asked.

He tilted his head to one side and scowled. "I tell you I love you and don't want to live without you, and instead of telling me you love me or at least giving me a reason…"

"Don't get all pissed off. I love you, too."

There she'd said it. Out loud. She waited for panic to set in, for her to begin stammering and trying to take it back. But none of that happened. Instead, it felt as natural as breathing.

"You do?"

She grinned and nodded. "I do, and I have no idea why because all of this is way too fast… but I need to call my boss. There are people I work with…"

"Not to worry. I called around and found your company. I found the San Francisco office number and spoke with Judith. She made a rather snarky remark about you having the luck of a cat with nine lives but told me to keep her informed as to your progress."

"Oh, thank god. She can be a bit much, but she's been a good friend. Now, let's get back to you telling me you love me."

He laughed out loud. "I thought we were talking about how much you deserve and need a spanking."

"Your words, not mine. Doc said I should take it easy."

"He did, but I don't think he meant for the rest of your life." Asher swung his legs up onto the bed, so he was leaning against the footboard looking at her. "Given that I think we want the same thing…"

"Can you transfer down to some place close to Gig Harbor? My office is in Seattle, but my home is in Gig Harbor. I take the passenger-only ferry—it's really a hydrofoil—to work every day."

Asher rubbed his chin and mouth, thinking. "I could probably get a transfer. No chance you could work remotely from Kodiak?"

"I don't think so. The Seattle branch is mainly just me and my office staff of one. You don't want to leave."

"No, but I want to lose you even less."

She couldn't exactly see Asher living in the lower forty-eight as he called it, and there was something about this place, and especially this man, that made her want to rethink her future plans.

"Can we table that for right now? Honestly, thinking about it makes my head hurt."

"We can table the details for right now, but I want to know that you're committed to making a life with me. As I say that out loud, I know how unreasonable that sounds."

"Really? I think it sounds sexy as hell. I keep turning it over in my mind, wondering how I can be so sure of my feelings. I keep thinking it's crazy for me to feel this way about a man I've known for basically a day—since I don't think being unconscious counts— but I am." She said the last with a little shrug.

Asher swung around on the bed and pulled her into his arms. "We'll make it work for both of us... I promise."

There was a knock on the door before a pretty blonde burst in. "Asher, I'm sorry to just come barging in. Hi, Nicole; I'm Betty; I work here. Ash, Jax needs you. Apparently, there's been some kind of accident. A couple of people are badly hurt. We're going to need all the rooms in here. Jax is going to put some volunteers at his house in town. And Trudy is putting up the people who aren't hurt. Even Colby is offering to help..."

"In other words, there is literally no room at the inn and we're going to need to hole up at Wolf Run."

"I'm afraid so. I'm sorry. I know things aren't good between you and your sire."

"No, but it is what it is. I'll see what I can do for Jax, and I'll let them know at Wolf Run that we'll be there for a couple of days. I'll need to call in to Randy, as well." He kissed Nicole. "Will you be all right until I get back?"

"Absolutely. I'd say I'll get my things packed, but I don't have any."

"Not true. Betty went to the mercantile for you and picked up some things."

"Thank you, Betty," said Nicole.

"No problem. Ash, Jax is out front."

"Go," said Nicole. "I'm fine. And if that changes, I'm right here at Doc's."

"I love you," he said, giving her a hard kiss and heading through the door.

She watched him go. Nicole knew she needed to get used to his going out, braving the elements, rescuing people and just in general doing his job. She hated to admit it, but she had no idea what all that entailed, but then he probably didn't know about hers, either.

"He's a good man," said Betty.

"I know. I'm head over heels for him, which makes no sense at all."

"It does to folks who know him. I need…"

"You need to go. You have things to do. I'll try and gather together any of the stuff that's mine or Ash's and go out to your waiting room… you have a waiting room, right?"

Betty smiled. "We do. Thanks, Nicole. I'll look forward to getting to know you."

Betty exited the room and Nicole sat for a moment. It seemed everyone, or at least Betty, expected her to uproot her life. Again, as with the 'I love you,' she expected to feel unsure or panicked or even resentful, but she didn't. It seemed that the presence she felt throughout her recovery was indeed Asher, and at some point her heart and soul must have committed her to him.

She swung her legs over the side of the bed and stood up gingerly, expecting pain, stiffness or at least some discomfort. There was none to be had. In fact, other than feeling a little weak, she felt better than she had in a long time.

She got dressed and then moved around the room, looking to see what she needed to put together. There wasn't much to gather. She could see where someone must have brought him a change of clothes and so she put what little they had in the duffle bag, picked up her ice tools, which someone had made sure were wiped down, and went looking for the waiting room.

As she came out snowmobiles were rushing up and people were being brought in. Betty was calm, cool, competent, and completely overwhelmed. Nicole put her things behind the reception desk. "You go do your triage or whatever you call it. I'll get people's names and emergency contacts."

"You just woke up…"

"But I feel great. A little weak, but honestly, I promise I won't overtax myself."

Betty squeezed her arm. "You're an angel. I can see why Asher fell for you."

For the next three hours, Betty, Doc, and Nicole worked like a well-oiled machine. At one point a handsome guy named Scott Hardaway who was a baker and caterer arrived with food, coffee, and goodies for everyone.

"The diner is trying to keep all of the volunteers fed. I told them I'd get food and coffee to all of you. Ash said to tell you I saw him and he's fine. Someone will be here soon from Wolf Run for you."

"Tell them to stay home. I'll go with Asher. Until then I'm needed here."

Scott grinned. "Good girl. Why don't you take a break and get something to eat. I'll watch over things here."

"I'm used to eating at my desk. I'm fine. In fact, I feel better now than I did when I started. Go take food and coffee to Betty and Doc. They're working a lot harder than I am."

"Yes, ma'am," he said, saluting her.

"I'm so sorry. Here you are helping out and I'm barking orders."

"Not to worry. At times like this, it's best to have people take charge to make sure it all gets done. I'll make sure everyone gets fed."

It was another two hours before the towering man who was Ash's father came barging through the door.

"Let's go," he said without preamble.

"I'm busy," Nicole said, making sure one of the patients who had been hurt, but not so badly that she'd been seen yet, was warm and had everything she needed.

"I said, let's go," he said, wrapping his hand around her arm.

She could feel Asher's presence and his anger before he entered the room from the back. "Take your hands off her," he growled in a low voice.

"She just woke up and she's working her fingers to the bone while you go off doing whatever it is you do," his father snarled back.

Nicole wrenched her arm away. "Are you this much of an asshole to everyone or just your son?"

"You keep out of this, girl," his father snapped at her.

"You," she said poking him in the chest, "get out of my waiting room."

"Why you…" he brought his hand back as if he meant to slap her. Nicole saw a blur of red as her ice axe sailed past her, sinking into the door frame, pinning him by his coat sleeve.

Before Ash's father could free himself, Ash had

closed the distance between them and had him by the throat, up against the wall. "Touch her again—ever—and you die. Do I make myself clear, old man?" He glanced over his shoulder for only a moment, not wanting to take his eyes off his father. "We'll need to make arrangements to stay somewhere other than Wolf Run."

"Don't be silly," said a beautiful older woman as she walked into the waiting room. She looked up at Nicole and smiled. "It would seem our prodigal son has returned with a beautiful woman. Honestly, men…" she said shaking her head and dislodging the ice axe. "You can live with them, but it's awful trying to live without them. I'm Gemma, mother to the younger hothead and wife to the older one."

She turned to Asher. "Decide what you want to do —kill him or let him go." Ash gave his father a shove for good measure and backed away. Gemma stepped between her mate and her son. "As for you, apologize to both of them and to all the other people you scared half to death."

"You don't tell me what to do," Ash's father growled.

"I do when you're being a jackass. Seriously, Ellis, the two of you bring out the absolute worst in each other."

"I won't have you leading me around by my dick. I am alpha…"

"And right now, you're being an alphahole.

There's been a serious accident, in case you missed it. Your son is saving people's lives, and his woman almost died but is here trying to help people."

"I was just trying to get her up to Wolf Run so she could rest."

"Bullshit," snarled Asher, the anger rolling off of him in waves.

"That's enough, Asher. We both know what your father was trying to do. In his own way, he was trying to be nice. I'm going to leave my vehicle here. Your father wants the doc and Jax to know that we have space at Wolf Run. Your father is going to drive me home now, so we can make sure we're ready. I'm going to assume Nicole will be sharing your room."

"I was not going to do any of those things," Ellis Wells said.

"No, but you will now because you love me and you love your son. I'm telling both of you, you can spend the night in one of the outbuildings if you don't play nice. Please, Ellis?"

"Well, I suppose." he grumbled, kissing Gemma. "Let us know when you're on your way. Let the sheriff know we can help if he needs us to, and we'll keep the roads clear north of town. I talked to Colby and he's doing the same to the south."

Asher nodded but said nothing.

Gemma turned to Nicole. "I do hope we don't spend your whole visit keeping these two from tearing each other apart."

Nicole smiled. "Me, too."

Ellis Wells kissed his wife again, adjusted her coat to keep her warm, and wrapped his arm around her waist and led her out the door.

"Your dad's a jackass, but I like your mom."

"Trust me, I know the feeling. I'm going to be a couple of hours more. If you want to go on up, Betty just took the last person into the back."

"I didn't even notice…"

"When my father goes on a rampage, it's best to keep your eye on him."

"Good shot with the ice axe."

"Not really. I was aiming for his shoulder to sever his arm and watch him bleed out."

She swatted his arm. "Asher Wells, that's a terrible thing to say. Think how your mom would feel and the mess you would have made."

Asher laughed. "Seriously, let me call them back. Doc's worried about you. I am, too. You're looking pale."

He opened the door to the outside. Nicole bit back a laugh. His father was sitting angrily in an SUV and his mother was standing right outside the door.

"We'll take good care of her; I promise. Please come with us, Nicole; you've been through a lot. Asher will feel better knowing you're safe and cared for."

Realizing she was far more tired than she'd allowed herself to believe, she nodded and started to walk past Ash. He stopped and kissed her before escorting her and his mother into the SUV. As they pulled away, she looked back to see him watching her. He trusted his mother, but it was clear there were old wounds and bad feelings between his father and him. She'd need to get to the bottom of that and make it clear to Wells senior that she would not allow him to hurt Ash any longer. If that meant they never came to Mystic River again, so be it.

NICOLE

She couldn't believe how exhausted she was. The last time she'd been this tired, she'd nearly frozen to death.

"He'll be fine. They've got all the people from the accident," said Gemma, twisting in her seat so she could smile at Nicole.

"Damn fools," snarled Ellis.

Gemma slapped at her husband's arm. "Don't mind him. He was looking forward to an easy evening, and then this came up."

"What happened?" asked Nicole.

"There was a private train with a small group of tourists. They shouldn't have tried to continue their journey on the tracks, but they did…"

"As I said, damn fools."

"Ellis," Ash's mother said with a patient tone. "Nicole is special to our son. Let's not give her cause to think she isn't welcome or that there's bad blood between you and Ash."

"There isn't. He's just too damn proud for his own good. I don't understand his need to play at being a hero."

That was it. She'd heard just about enough from Ash's father as she was going to.

"Your son doesn't play at being a hero. He served his country with honor and distinction as a SEAL and then he joined the rangers to protect our national parks, the environment, and the damn fools, as you like to call them, when they get into trouble. I think you might be the only father who wouldn't be proud of his son. Guess the term damn fool fits you as well."

"How dare you," Ellis started.

"I dare because I love your son and in case you missed it, I'm not in the least bit afraid of you."

"And you call me the fool?"

"I do. You can't be so stupid as to think if you did anything to harm me, your son wouldn't rip you limb from limb…"

"She has a point," inserted Gemma.

Ellis grumbled something that Nicole couldn't quite hear.

"If you think I'll let you talk shit about the man I love, you couldn't be more wrong. So, if that's what I'm going to be subjected to, you can just turn around and take me back to town. Ash and I will find someplace else to stay."

"No one wants that, Nicole," said Gemma soothingly.

Nicole returned her smile and shook her head gently—mainly because anything else would make her head hurt worse. "Have you always had to play peacemaker between them?"

"I'm afraid so. The fact is, they are too much alike." Ellis made a growling sound. "Get used to that noise when you point out the obvious. They've had what could be charitably called a volatile relationship since Ash was about five. He's always known what he wanted…"

"And didn't give a damn what anyone thought about it. He just ran off and did what he wanted…"

Gemma arched her eyebrow at him, before looking back at Nicole. "As I said, like father like son."

"No, he's your son. You've coddled him since he was a baby."

"You're right, when he was a little boy I protected him as any mother would do. And if he's my son, it's because you never made him feel he was anything but a disappointment to you."

"I let him join the damn Navy with his two friends, Jax and Colby, didn't I? Went to the damn ceremony when he became a SEAL…"

"Only because I threatened to go without you and do some shopping, so you'd be sleeping by yourself." She grinned at Nicole. "That's another way father and son are alike…"

Surprisingly, Nicole was certain that Ellis Wells blushed. It was kind of cute and endearing.

"For pity's sake, Gemma, you don't say things like that in front of someone who isn't a part of our pack."

Pack? That wasn't the first time someone had made a reference to a pack.

"If you're going to behave badly around her and claim she has to forgive you as she will be family, then I suggest you start showing her the better side of your personality, so she wants to be. Don't make Asher choose between her and us. I don't think you'll like the decision he makes. Please forgive my husband, Nicole."

"I don't need you making apologies for me."

"I'd let her if I were you," quipped Nicole. "I'm not sure you could apologize your way out of a brown paper sack. She's rather good at them. But then, my guess is she's had lots of practice."

Gemma laughed. "I really think you and I are going to get along well."

"I have no doubt about that, but the grouch you married is going to have to work at it."

Ellis might have said something more, but they turned into a grand driveway with an enormous gate with an ornate sign overhead of a pack of wolves running and the name of Ash's boyhood home, Wolf Run.

He hit the button on some kind of automatic

opener and the gates slowly swung open. There was a brick perimeter wall, so the estate's lush beauty had been hidden.

"This is gorgeous," Nicole said, looking out on the snowy landscape.

"It is pretty," said Gemma, smiling. "I remember when Ellis first brought me here. I thought it was the most beautiful place I'd ever seen. I've been here for more than thirty years, and my opinion hasn't changed. I called ahead to have them freshen up Asher's room. It's upstairs at the other end of the hall from our suite."

"Damn waste of space, if you ask me," grumbled Ellis.

"I don't believe anyone did," said Gemma, her patience beginning to wear thin. "He is our son and the heir to Wolf Run. He and Nicole will rule here one day, God willing, and you must find a way to make peace with him."

"I'm not the one who left."

"No. You just made sure he didn't feel welcome when he came home. I really doubt he would have left again after the SEALs if you hadn't made it untenable for him here."

"Jax and Colby stayed."

"Jax became sheriff and Colby is a gangster, and neither had a father who behaved so badly even his beta admonished him in private."

Ellis' head snapped around to look at his wife. "How do you know about that?"

"I know a great many things of which you are unaware. My hope is our son learned from your mistakes and will be more forthcoming with Nicole. Now you be nice."

Ellis shook his head and then smiled. Nicole had never thought a smile could change someone's features the way his did.

"Thirty plus years and you're still the same sassy brat I put over my knee that first time."

Gemma leaned over, placing both of her hands on her husband's thigh and kissed his cheek. "I remember. You wouldn't have me any other way."

Ellis chuckled. "No. I don't suppose I would."

"I'm sure a lot of our people are going to have figured out a reason to be up at the main house. I know Asher and the doctor want you to rest. I'm going to sort of usher you through the crowd and take you upstairs. Betty was kind enough to give me your sizes, so I bought you a few things. Hopefully, we can make you feel comfortable and welcome."

"You've already done that, Gemma. I am tired, so if I could just lie down until Asher gets here, that would be great." Her stomach made a grumbling noise. It had been a while since she'd last eaten.

"How about I bring you up a tray with something to munch on. Dinner has been served so when Ash arrives, I'll see that you both get something more substantial unless you'd rather have that now."

"No, I'd rather wait for Asher. Is there a bath close to his room?"

Gemma smiled. "Asher's room is actually a suite. It's not quite as large as his father's and mine, but it has a lovely wraparound balcony and an attached bath with a shower and separate tub."

"A tub," Nicole sighed wistfully.

"Food or soak first? Or both at the same time?"

"That would be decadent…"

"There is absolutely nothing wrong with decadent."

Gemma proved to be right. There seemed to be an inordinate amount of people milling around the front entrance, which was four steps up to a large portico. Instead of lions sitting atop a set of decorative columns, there were wolves. It made sense. After all the place was called Wolf Run.

Ellis opened both of their doors to help them out and Gemma linked her arm through Nicole's, leading her up the stairs through a large foyer and then up a main staircase and down the hall to Asher's suite. It had double doors and the view when they were opened was amazing. It seemed as if the entire back wall consisted of an enormous fireplace flanked by a bank of floor to ceiling windows on either side. Opposite it on the interior wall was a large bed, positioned so that the occupants thereof had a magnificent view of the fireplace and the forest and hills that lay beyond.

"This is gorgeous. Don't get me wrong; the cabin is beautiful…"

"But you can't beat the view," Gemma finished with a knowing look.

Gemma made sure that Nicole knew where everything was and then left her to rest and snack on the plate that had been waiting for their arrival. Asher's mother closed the door behind her as she left, and Nicole made short work of getting rid of her clothes, putting them in the large laundry basket inside the walk-in closet. It was easy to tell where Asher had gotten his sense of design.

Nicole ran a tub of hot, scented water. She found several bath oils to choose from and smiled. It was obvious Gemma had gone to some trouble to make her feel welcome, despite her grumpy husband. She set the tray of food down on a shelf by the tub that looked to be designed for just that. Head back, she closed her eyes and allowed the water to work its magic. When she'd allowed herself a good soak, she got out of the tub, dried off and wrapped a luxurious robe around her body and sat in one of two wingback chairs in front of the fireplace.

As she had at the clinic, she could feel Asher's presence before he entered the room. She lifted her arms and welcomed him into them as he knelt beside her, kissing her with a pent-up passion.

"Hello, lover. I missed you," she said when he finally allowed her to come up for air.

"I see my mother's been looking after you. Remind me to thank her for that. You look like you're feeling better."

"I am. I took a nice long soak in your tub and have just been sitting here by the fire pondering the future."

"Made any decisions?"

"Only one, but several observations."

"What are the observations?" he asked lifting her out of the chair, sitting down, and settling her in his lap.

"Your father's an ass."

Asher laughed. "I understand you told him that in no uncertain terms. My mother adores you and thinks you're perfect for me."

"And your father?"

"He thinks you need to have a strap taken to your backside."

"What do you think?" she asked, feeling there was more weight to the question than teasing.

"I think he's right, although maybe not a strap as I doubt anyone has ever corrected your behavior. But I made a deal with the powers that be that I'd let it slide unless you gave me leave to do otherwise."

"Would it hurt?"

He nodded. "A discipline spanking is just that—punishment." He chuckled, "But given the way your arousal ticks up every time we talk about it, I'm sure it'll end in a rather righteous lovemaking session."

Nicole thought for a moment before asking. "Will it make it easier for you to accept my apology and not let it simmer between us?"

"Yes, and I think it will do the same for you. Both of us will know you've accepted responsibility for what you did, acceded to my authority, and atoned for your behavior."

"Then yes… if that's going to be the way we go, we may as well start the same."

She could tell he was surprised by her answer. Truth to tell, so was she. She couldn't say she was looking forward to feeling Asher's strong hands tattooing her backside with his displeasure, but she had a bad habit of allowing things to fester so getting them dealt with in a way both people agreed to seemed like a better idea.

"I think we need to give you a day or two to make sure you're all right."

"I'm fine. Really. After that soak and my nap here by the fire, I feel better than I have in years. I'd rather get this over with and be able to move forward. I don't want to let my anxiety get the better of me."

"I can appreciate that." He helped her off his lap and stood. "In that case, hand me the robe, Nicole."

Her entire body went from warm and relaxed to trembling with need in the space of a heartbeat. There was something about Asher Wells—something that made everything with him seem right and natural. She untied the robe, slid out of it, and handed it to him. Somehow, she knew, it was more than the robe that he'd demanded she surrender. She knew she was handing him her future. Her destiny was inexplicably intertwined with his. What that might look like or entail, she hadn't a clue. All she knew was that in that moment, she surrendered her heart, mind, body, and soul into his keeping.

CHAPTER 15

NICOLE

There was something about standing naked in nothing but the light of the moon beaming through the window and the light cast from the large fireplace that made her arousal spike and made her feel beautiful. Asher had a way of looking at her and trailing his fingers across her skin that was possessive and seductive at the same time. His hands traced the curves of her body that he had come to know intimately the night before she made her disastrous climb.

He walked around her, maintaining physical contact with her as he rumbled a sound from deep within him. She could feel it wash over her, caressing every fiber in her being and firing every synapse. It was as if her body had been on autopilot before and now was coming fully online in a way it never had.

Asher stopped before her and brought both hands

up her sides to cup and weigh the lush heaviness of her breasts before allowing his thumbs to strum across her nipples, teasing them into pebbled peaks. One hand left her breast and moved around her side to the base of her spine before gliding up to the nape of her neck. He moved his hand so he fisted her hair from beneath it, tilting her head back so his mouth could capture hers.

He fused his lips to hers, which parted in both submission and invitation. Asher plunged his tongue deep inside to find and dance with hers. His fingers tightened in her hair, and he twisted it to hold her head immobile. There were no two ways about it—the man knew how to kiss. He continued to kiss her. When she thought to bring her hands up to touch him, he growled into her mouth and tweaked her nipple. When her eyes flew open, they locked with his, intent upon her. He continued to pinch her tightly beaded tip, increasing the pressure until she dropped her hands.

The instant she acquiesced, the pressure was released, and he went back to leisurely exploring her body as he deepened and intensified the pleasure of his kisses. As he continued to kiss and play with her nipples and breasts, she could feel her molten core beginning to pool and spread its warmth throughout her body.

His hands left her breast to remove his sweater; he released her hair only long enough to pull it away. He retook her mouth, and her breath as well, as his hand sank once more into her tresses and pulled down on them. She opened her eyes and again found herself staring into fathomless orbs of dark brown tinged with a kind of eternal fire lurking behind them and all around the edges.

Asher tugged on her hair again. "On your knees," he commanded softly.

She found it easy to kneel in front of him. Without releasing his hold on her hair, he used his other hand to unbutton the fly of his jeans and release his engorged cock, presenting it to her. Nicole leaned forward and ran her tongue along the notch at his hip that pointed straight to his staff.

When she reached up to wrap her hand around it, he tugged her hair. "No hands."

She grinned. She'd forgotten how much he enjoyed being in control, which was fine with her as he knew his way around her body, and no one had ever given her more pleasure. She enveloped the head of his cock with her mouth as he pressed forward, trying to use her tongue to trace the contours and veins. Asher all but ignored her ministrations as he moved in and out, groaning with the exquisite pleasure he took from both her submission and desire.

He slid from her mouth and tugged upward on her hair, giving her his other hand to help her rise.

"I'm so fucked, aren't I?" she managed to whisper.

"Not yet, but you will be—often and well," he

added with a grin as he backed toward the bed, pulling one of the large pillows at the head down about midway and then helping her to lie across it so that it supported her hips, making her ass the highest point of her body. "Did you deliberately cause me to believe you were not going to try and climb Pyramid Mountain on your own?"

She hesitated, not entirely sure she knew what he wanted. When his hand smacked her ass, the answer became very clear.

"Yes."

"Yes, Sir, when you're being punished." His hand landed again, making Nicole gasp at the heat and pain that bloomed from the contact.

"Yes, Sir."

"Better. And did your misbehavior almost get you killed?"

"Yes, Sir. I am sorry, Ash."

"Not as sorry as you will be," he said as he landed a flurry of stinging swats all across her backside.

Nicole wasn't sure which was worse, the actual pain from the spanking or the humiliation that she felt from the arousal it seemed to ignite. Another five smacks and he stopped, softly rubbing the affected area.

"Spread your legs."

Sighing and burying her face in the bed clothes, she did as she was told. His hand slipped between her legs—his fingers tracing sensual designs along the insides of her thighs before they stroked her wet pussy, removing the moisture he found there to rub into her clit. Over and over, he moved his hand—rubbing, stroking, caressing her pussy, clit and back to the puckered rose hiding in the cleft of her ass.

Nicole moaned, not from pain, but from the arousal and need that flowed through her being. Her breathing was losing its steady rhythm, becoming thready and shallow.

He smacked her again and again on each cheek and then landed one to her swollen and wet pussy. The blows still stung, especially the ones to her sex, but it wasn't pain she registered—just a new kind of caress she'd never experienced before. Her hips were moving, undulating in an old rhythm that was an invitation for him to bury his cock deep inside her.

"Please, Ash."

She could hear him pushing his jeans down past his hips and thighs as he took the place he had already claimed as his between her legs. The feel of his flesh against hers was a caress in and of itself as he pressed the head of his cock against the entrance to her core. He barely entered her before stopping. Grasping her hips in his hands, he surged forward in a single, ruthless thrust, groaning with pleasure as he did so.

He remained deep inside her for a moment, reveling in the way her pussy spasmed all along his length before drawing back and then driving home again. He drew back and then surged in again, setting up a pounding rhythm as he did so.

He'd fucked her from behind before, but it was nothing like this. Each and every time he thrust into her, his hard thighs met her tender buttocks. Instead of detracting from the pleasure, it increased it, ramping up the sensations of being possessed and claimed by him. It was almost surreal. She'd only known Ash less than a week, and yet felt she had known him her whole life and probably several more lifetimes before this one.

The swell of her orgasm began to build, and its power made her tremble at his touch. It washed over her with the strength of a tsunami, making her cry out his name as the waves rippled over her in a kind of never-ending pleasure.

Asher groaned, hammering her pussy with several merciless thrusts until he ground against her, the warm rush of his release bathing her tender flesh. He held himself pressed deep inside her as he emptied the torrent of his cum within.

He collapsed on her back for a moment before rolling them both to their sides, his cock still within her.

"God, I love you," he whispered.

Nicole snuggled back against him. "I love you, too, and I am so sorry for all of it."

"It's done, sweetheart. You're alive. We're

together. You screwed up. I disciplined you and that's the end of it."

He sat up only long enough to remove his boots, socks, and jeans before settling behind her, his front spooned to her back as he wrapped his arms around her. Nicole had never felt so satiated, warm, and loved.

She awoke sometime later still wrapped in Asher's arms, his breath warm on the back of her neck. Betty had given her some bandages for the wound on her neck but said unless it started bleeding to leave it until at least tomorrow. Nicole eased out of Ash's embrace and bed and padded quietly into the bath. It was nice that they had an attached private bath. It meant she didn't have to throw on a robe to use it.

It was funny that Kevin had never liked her being nude. They both slept in pajamas and were always covered up even when it was just the two of them. When she'd gotten her divorce, she had indulged in a couple of very pretty nightgowns and a chenille and paisley robe, but she rarely wore any of them anymore. Her house was very private, and she was no longer ashamed of her curves. She smiled when she remembered how Ash had praised her voluptuous figure and made her believe she was the most beautiful thing he'd ever seen.

She turned on the light and saw the bandage had a small dot of blood on it. No doubt that had been the result of their lovemaking. She didn't care. Doc could fuss and scold all he wanted… Ash could too for that matter.

He'd been right about the spanking. It had settled something deep between them. To think a spanking could have such a profound effect on her seemed ludicrous, and yet it had. She had been fairly convinced that she was willing to do whatever it took to be with Ash, and now there was no doubt in her mind. There was no doubt that he was a dominant alpha male and she realized that so many who claimed to be had no clue whatsoever. So many women were so hungry for a man with whom they could share their lives but who would take on a position of leadership that they would believe any idiot who knew how to espouse the right words.

Thinking back, she realized Kevin had been one of them. He wanted control for the sake of being in control but wanted to delegate all of the real work in their relationship to her. Asher, on the other hand, wanted to ease her burdens and make her life easier. Yes, he needed control, but only in certain areas, and he didn't see her as weak if she wanted to let him lead. There were times she got so weary.

She carefully removed the tape from the four sides of the bandage and then soaked the bandage itself so she could easily remove it. She could feel the bandage release and she removed it, seeing the wound for the first time.

Her eyes widened, her heart skipped a beat and

she had to remind herself to breathe. Nicole stared into the mirror at the distinctive wound—four evenly spaced holes from deep punctures with a series of six more shallow punctures. It was a bite mark. It seemed to be healing well. The blood appeared to be from the teeth between the fangs.

Someone had bitten her. The dregs of memory stirred, vague and imprecise, but unmistakable. Not someone.

Asher.

Asher had bitten her. Why? That was a stupid question. Little bits and pieces of things he'd said, things that had somehow permeated her state of unconsciousness and remained within her memory, an estate called Wolf Run…the pieces began falling into place.

She turned her back to the mirror, leaning against the vanity to steady herself. Could there really be wolf-shifters in the world? If so, were there other kinds of shifters? If Asher was a wolf-shifter, then his parents had to be wolf-shifters as well. Hadn't somebody referred to those at Wolf Run as a pack?

Her thoughts were jumbled, and Nicole tried to make sense of them. No matter which way she turned them around, she kept coming back to the one conclusion that—in its own weird way—made the most sense. Asher was a wolf-shifter and had bitten her, which if Maddie Owen knew what she was talking about, also meant that he'd made her one too without her consent.

She waited to feel outraged, but she didn't. If Asher had turned her without asking her, he must have believed she was on death's very doorstep. He'd done it to save her life. Initiating the shift in her DNA would also explain why she'd been unconscious. It wasn't so much that she was recovering as it was that her body was going through the transition.

Nicole stifled a giggle. She never giggled. She hadn't giggled since she was five. She laughed, but she didn't giggle. She remembered reading an interview with Maddie Owen where the book blogger didn't like paranormal romances and was attacking her books.

He'd finally asked her, "Do you believe in the absurd possibilities you write about?"

Maddie had responded, "We know for a fact that nature allows for the absurd—just look at giraffes and ostriches. As for possibilities? I like to believe in the magic that all things and creatures are possible."

She'd bet anything that Maddie Owen knew it for a fact and wondered if perhaps her favorite author might have so much insight because she was one.

Asher appeared in the doorway. He started to say something, but his eyes became riveted to the wound on her neck.

"I can explain…"

She shook her head. "No need to. You're a wolf,

or rather a wolf-shifter, and I'm one now, too, aren't I?"

CHAPTER 16

ASHER

He'd meant to tell her. He wanted to bind her to him, to make her believe he loved her and to trust that he would never do anything to harm her. He stared at the wound. It seemed to be healing well. He wondered why she had removed the bandage. The claiming bite, for that's what it was, and she would need to accept that, would leave a pronounced scar, as Asher was an alpha male wolf.

A few more days and he would have explained everything to her, but now time had caught him up and he could do nothing more than try to talk to her and keep her from panicking. Even as the thought crossed his mind, Asher realized there was no danger of Nicole panicking. In fact, everything about her seemed calm—calm, happy, and peaceful.

"That idea doesn't seem to be something you're having trouble accepting," he said, slowly.

"Answer my question."

He walked towards her, raising his arms to pull her close. He expected her to push him away, wince, or outright reject him. Instead, she came willingly, wrapping her arms around his waist and laying her head on his chest.

"Yes," he said finally.

She laughed. It wasn't so much that he could hear the sound as he could feel it in the way her body shook, and her breath raced across his skin in delighted puffs.

"I have so many questions and you are going to answer all of them."

He agreed, his chin dipping in acquiescence. "But first, you will answer one of mine."

"Just one and then I get to ask all the ones I want?" He nodded again, looking directly into her eyes. There was no evasion hiding in their depths. "All right, then, what's the question?"

He stepped back from her and sank to one knee. "Nicole Sullivan, will you marry me?"

The myriad of emotions that danced across her face reminded him of the way the Aurora Borealis moved and flowed, changing color, speed, and rhythm. He let out a breath he didn't know he was holding when she settled on a smile.

"Yes, Asher Wells, I will marry you."

She'd said yes. She'd actually said yes. Asher had expected at the very least an argument if not an outright fight. Allowing love, elation, and relief to surge to the forefront of his emotions and before she could continue or change her mind, he stood up, swept her up in his arms and twirled her around. Nicole threw back her head and laughed as he carried her out into the main room and settled them in the wingback chair by the fireplace.

"You won't regret it, Nicole. I swear it. How did you know? Why aren't you more freaked out?"

She laughed, tilting her head so she could see him better. "Did you want me to be frightened?"

"Of course, not. But I have to tell you that your reaction is a bit…" he hesitated, looking for the right word, "unique."

"For the record, you've used up your one question, but I'm feeling benevolent and incredibly happy. So, how did I know? I told you I'm a huge fan of Maddie Owen's."

Asher groaned. "You need to know, she's not exactly popular with our kind."

"Is she in danger writing what she does?"

"She might have been had she not become the mate to a powerful alpha with even more powerful friends. Anyone who wants to go after Maddie, they'd have to go through Griffin Owen and the Coalition—eight packs who formed an alliance during one of our darkest times. Not something any sane wolf would do."

"Well, Maddie describes the bite mark and its location. I'm going to make the benign assumption that you didn't just turn me for fun…"

"I would never," he growled low.

Nicole silenced his growl by kissing him. "Of course, you wouldn't. And I would never have thought that, which leads me to what I was going to say, which was that I'm guessing I was close to death when you got to me…"

"I don't want to mislead you. I wanted you to stay the weekend to get closer to you with the eye to establishing a strong bond where I could talk to you and convince you to become one with me."

"Please tell me the part about not having to worry about gaining weight isn't something she made up, because I'd really like that."

He laughed out loud. "It is far easier for our kind to maintain their weight, but don't start thinking about losing weight. You are perfect just the way you are."

"Thank God. As for how I knew, the bite mark of course, which allowed bits and pieces I'd overheard to fall into place. I take it you are an alpha wolf?"

"I am."

"So, this sucker," she said, touching the wound gingerly with her fingertips, "is going to leave a scar."

"It is."

"No apology for that? Just yep, it's going to leave a scar?" she quipped.

"A prominent one."

"And that doesn't bother you?"

Asher began to relax. She really was taking this much better than he'd ever dreamed she would. He hadn't been transparently honest with the information from the first, but he vowed not to ever do that to her again. Not telling her he was a wolf-shifter when they first met was apparently something she could forgive, but he didn't want to take his chances with not being open with her from now on. "Not one damn bit."

"Why?"

"Because to any other kind of shifter, it's a kind of *no trespassing* sign. Especially another wolf-shifter. If you've read Maddie's books you know male alpha wolves are notoriously territorial."

"Yes, she makes the point that they aren't jealous, but they don't like other men messing with what they consider theirs."

"Precisely. Is reading Maddie's books why you aren't as bothered by the idea that I took your humanity?"

"As opposed to what, letting me die?" she said, her head shaking in a quick but decisive no. "Hot news flash: I don't want to die, at least not until I've lived a full life. I think reading Maddie's books gave me more insight into what I'm getting myself into. Was she turned?"

"Yes, by Griffin and with her full consent. She'd found out about us on a trip to London, where she was almost abducted by a pack looking for human females to turn and either use for their own pack or to sell off to others." She frowned. "As I said, a dark time for our species."

"So, your…"

"Our," he corrected.

She grinned. "Our kind came into being by evolving right alongside humans on a different evolutionary path, but always hiding in plain sight."

"Not always. There was a time humans and shifters lived alongside each other, facing the dangers of early life with a united front. But as humans became more sophisticated, they became more distrusting and covetous of our abilities. After all, being able to shift into an animal gave us an edge and made us better suited to some environments. And where we could change humans to shifters, they could not change shifters to humans."

"So, they were jealous…"

"In some ways, but I also think understandably. Our numbers weren't as great as the humans and most shifters don't intermingle with other shifters. In the end, shifters were persecuted, often being labeled witches and burned at the stake. So, we withdrew from the world of humans. But as the human population spread and intruded on our territories and habitats, we learned to adapt and then to live alongside them."

"I'm so sorry…"

"You didn't do anything wrong, sweetheart."

"Is everyone at Wolf Run a shifter?"

"Everyone in Mystic River, unless they're visitors or there's some kind of emergency, is a shifter. Everyone at Wolf Run is a wolf-shifter. My father is alpha."

"Of course, he is. He is also a jerk."

Asher chuckled. "Agreed."

"Doc and Betty?"

He grinned. "Fox-shifters."

He hadn't expected it would be such a relief to tell her everything. Some of the citizens of Mystic River might not like that he'd told her, but Asher didn't care. He knew without a doubt that she would never betray them.

"Scott Hardaway?" she asked.

"He and Kyra Reynolds, the town's deputy, as well as Kyra's older brother, Colby, are lynx-shifters. Colby is the alpha of their clowder, and they have an estate at the other end of town called Windsong Manor. Traditionally, shifters have kept to their own kind. But when Mystic River was founded, Alaska was a wild and raw place, and the founders decided it was easier to co-exist together and form a community."

"Sheriff Miller?"

"Can't you guess?"

Nicole laughed. "Bear-shifter," she said, settling back into the comfort of his lap.

"Correct. A lot of the shifters have compounds similar to Wolf Run and Windsong, but not the bears. They can be loners, only banding together when they have to."

"Isn't being sheriff kind of an anomaly for him? The best sheriffs are the ones who care about the communities they serve."

"No one cares more about Mystic River than Jax. He is one of my oldest friends. When he returned from being a SEAL the community asked him to become sheriff and he did. He does a great job. People either respect or fear him, but either way, he's able to protect this town and its people."

"Was your mom always a wolf?"

"No. My dad turned her. No, he didn't have her consent, and yes, I will ensure that any of our children know that is a family tradition that ends with their parents."

"She seems to love him now."

Asher smiled. "My mother is a very tolerant person, and she does love him. Why I'm not sure, but she does. She might argue with him in private, but they always present a united front. She is also a most beloved mistress to the Mystic River Pack."

"Wait. Don't I recall reading that there are no wolves, at least none of the four-legged kind, on

Kodiak Island? Do you ever have a problem when you want to shift and run?"

"My father is opposed to our shifting. He worries that the risk is too great. The pack, as long as I can remember, has never run or hunted as wolves. Many of our people feel they are being slowly strangled, or at least homogenized, so they leave. He is alpha. I should inherit his title and position when he dies, but I'm not sure there will be a pack to inherit."

"The source of the bad blood between you?"

"Some of it. I never abided by my father's edict against shifting and did so on a regular basis. He felt I was a bad influence on some of the others and made my life a living hell. So, I left. Jax, Colby, and I joined the Navy and became SEALS."

"All three of you?"

He wagged his head. "No, just Jax and I. Colby joined Naval Intelligence, only on his last mission, he got bad intelligence and Jax's and my unit was wiped out, except for the two of us."

She was silent for a moment, taking that in. "Are there other wolf-shifters on Kodiak Island?"

"Centuries ago, but the other packs left the islands long before the formation of Mystic River. My family has been here since the beginning, but my father, in his infinite wisdom, refuses to modernize the way things are done and so the pack grows smaller as new wolves come along and chafe under the yoke of his leadership."

"Not that you have strong feelings about that," she teased.

"Sorry. As I'm sure you realized, there is bad blood between us. He resented my leaving to join the Navy…"

"Then why did you?"

"As I said, we never got along, and if I'd stayed, I'd have challenged him for leadership." Asher took a deep breath, exhaling it slowly. "He wouldn't have gone quietly, and I wouldn't have allowed him to stay and be a disruptive influence."

"You'd have banished your own father?" she asked.

Asher liked that it was simple curiosity and trying to understand in her tone. There was no judgement whatsoever.

"I doubt he would have accepted defeat. I would have had to kill him."

"Your mother…"

"Exactly. She would never have forgiven me, and rightfully so. Maddie Owen makes a big deal about the protectiveness of male wolves. Trust me, some of the most protective, vengeful, and deadly wolves I've ever known were she-wolves."

Nicole wrapped her arms around him, hugging him close. She said nothing, she didn't have to. They were bonded mates, and she knew his pain as surely as if it were her own. He'd never talked to anyone about the depths of his feelings regarding his leaving his pack. He suspected his mother knew, and Jax and Colby could probably guess.

"I have two more questions."

"Shoot."

"When can I learn to shift?"

He nuzzled her neck. "I knew you were my fated mate. I just knew it. What's the other?"

"Is Maddie telling the truth about the alpha knot?"

"The next time I see Griffin, remind me to punch him in the face for letting her write those books."

She grinned. "I'll take that as a yes."

"Indeed, but you need to be fully healed before that, and someone other than you needs to tell me that. As for shifting, if you're up to it, there's no time like the present."

CHAPTER 17

NICOLE

*N*icole leaped out of his lap, gleeful at the prospect of being able to shift from one form to another. In her books, Maddie Owen made the concept of being a wolf-shifter something to be envied. Nicole was certain that Maddie had embraced her she-wolf. There was such joy when she wrote about running through the wild and a deep sensuality and eroticism to the idea of the knot.

"I'm already naked. Does clothing really not survive the shift?" she asked, feeling almost giddy at the idea of her body becoming something else.

He snorted. "You may be the best-informed newbie she-wolf that ever lived. To answer your question, clothing does not survive a shift, but precious metals and jewels do. No one has ever been able to figure out why." He crossed the room to her, kissing her deeply. "I am madly in love with you, and you are going to make a beautiful she-wolf."

"I'm already naked," she repeated. "So, what do I do?"

"We'll get dressed and head down to the barn. I don't need to rub my father's nose in the fact that we're going to shift and go for a run. A lot of shifters have homes with door handles that can be manipulated in their animal form. As you can see, Wolf Run is not among them."

"We can just tell them we're going for a walk in the moonlight."

Mirth soaked Asher's expression, enhancing his dark, brooding good looks. "Come along, mate. God, I have wanted to call you that since we had lunch."

"Did you know?"

"Didn't you? You read Maddie's books. Didn't you have a buzzing in your head?"

"I've read that so many times. It never occurred to me that I was feeling the call of my fated mate. Will we get married, as well, like with a wedding?"

"Absolutely, I want you tied to me in as many ways as I can come up with."

They got dressed and then ventured down the stairs. The house was mostly quiet, and they managed to get out the back door without anyone seeing them. Asher led her down to the big barn, which was filled with gorgeous horses and equipment.

"They're beautiful. Does everyone ride?"

"Some do, but we also use them to get around the estate. So much nicer than a bunch of ATVs, although we do have some snowmobiles. My mother loves horses, so she prefers horse-drawn sleighs. One of the other outbuildings has a collection of carriages and sleighs. It's pretty impressive. Most of them were given to my mother by my father, usually when he'd been even more of a jerk than normal."

Nicole laughed. She could tell the rift between him and his father ran deep, and it caused him far more pain than he cared to admit. She rose up on her tiptoes and brushed her lips against his.

"Strip," he said without preamble.

"If you think I'm going to get naked and drop to my knees to give you a blow job, think again."

"Really?" he said, twisting his fingers in her black, curly mane and giving it a tug. "You should know that male alphas expect their mate to be available to them sexually at any time."

"Does that go the other way?" she teased.

"Absolutely. But I wouldn't ask you to do that in a freezing cold barn. Actually, we'll go in the tack room, which is heated, and we'll leave our clothes there, so we have something to put on when we shift back." He led her to the tack room, opening the door and closing it behind them. "I said strip."

Nicole could feel her lips lifting in a smile. She removed her clothing and was gratified and reassured as Asher took in the sight of her body and his body responded in a positive way.

"It's the cold," she said, glancing down at her stiffened nipples.

"No, it's not, but I'll take care of that when we get back up to our room. I want you to close your eyes and clear your mind. Think of the most peaceful place you've ever been. The place you feel the safest."

Her eyes flew open. "That would be your bed."

"Our bed," he corrected, trying to be stern as he covered his laugh. "Then picture the prettiest mountaintop you've ever been on. Breathe in that air, that sense of accomplishment. Let calm and courage be your constant companions."

Nicole did so, pulling up one of the beautiful valleys on Mt. Rainier. She could feel a sense of peace infusing her being.

"Now, look for your wolf. She should be lurking at the fringes of your mind. Do you see her?"

"Yes, she's beautiful. Wait. Should I talk?"

This time he could not contain his laughter. "You better because when you're a wolf, you don't have the right kind of vocal cords to form words. You can bark, yip, howl, and a lot of other vocalizations, but no words. Now close your eyes and concentrate. When you're first learning, calling her forward is something you have to be clearly intent on. There will come a time you can ask her to join with you or take over and she will." He put his hand on her shoulder. "You'll be able to see and feel a swirling mist that will surround you. You'll feel an electricity-like charge, see shards of color and hear thunder. It's all a part of the shift. Your wolf will gallop towards you and leap. She won't hurt you."

Nicole nodded. "I'm ready."

Just as Asher had told her and Maddie Owen had described, she could feel a kind of controlled chaos surround her. She'd always thought Maddie was a good writer, but her description of the shift paled in comparison to its reality. Thunder and lightning crackled and boomed all around her, mixed in with shards of color that were reminiscent of the Aurora Borealis.

Nicole looked to her wolf and saw the great beast galloping towards her, leaping at her so they could join and be one. She'd expected to feel some kind of change come over her—bones cracking, face elongating, something… but nothing came. All she felt was a sense of finally being whole. Then the mist fell away and she found herself on all fours, with a big bushy tail on the other end.

"God, you're beautiful," Asher sighed, running his hand down her silky coat, and then removed his own clothing before the swirling mist of fire and ice encompassed him and then he, too, was wolf.

He nosed open the door that he hadn't closed tightly behind them and trotted out into the barn. The horses seemed restless, which seemed odd as they lived with wolves, and then she remembered those at Wolf Run were not allowed to shift. Asher nuzzled her and then led her out of the building before picking up a trot.

It wasn't as instinctual as she thought it would be. Learning to use four legs instead of two was going to take some practice, and while Asher could wag his tail, when she tried, she fell over. She growled in frustration, and he nuzzled against her, letting his emotions flow and soothe her. They trotted down to a big field where he began to chase his tail. It looked like fun, so she tried to imitate him, and ended up tying herself in a knot and planting her face in the snow.

Asher came to her side, helping her regain her feet, and chased his tail again. When he stopped, he wagged his tail and woofed at her in a low tone. Clearly, he wanted her to make a fool of herself, but then again, maybe he was trying to teach her something. As she started, he stayed at her side, impeding her speed. Little by little, she began to feel more confident and sure-footed. He seemed to understand and pulled back so she could go faster.

The feeling was not at all dizzying. She spun one way, barking in her exuberance, and then tried to spin the other way, resulting in another face plant. She shook her head at him when he tried to coddle her and got to her feet. This time she began going slowly until she felt she had control of things. It was actually quite fun, and she could feel her wolf embracing her.

She stopped, sat in the snow, and looked at him, yapping happily at him. He whirled around and trotted off; she followed. Once she was able to match his speed at the trot, he began to lope, which she picked up far more quickly. The lope became a gallop as they crested the moonlit hill and began to run and play with each other.

Nicole had never run barefoot through the snow, but she rather imagined her human feet would not do as well as her wolf feet were doing. Aside from being freezing, the pads of her feet and the way they were formed gave her much better traction as they ran the fields.

She found it interesting that even though she couldn't speak, her mind functioned as it always had. It was almost as if she was sharing a brain and all of her senses with the wolf. She could feel the cold, rationally think about it, and yet she wasn't human. It was oddly disconnected and yet harmonious.

With a burst of speed, she knocked into Asher and then ran gleefully down a hill. She remembered doing something similar as a small child. When she reached the bottom, she whirled around, and play bowed to him. The instinct was what drove the physical, but the human part of her brain knew what it was. He woofed and then splatted at her feet, rolling onto his back and wallowing in the snow. She joined him. She could feel the cold of the ground, but not in an unpleasant way.

Asher jumped to his feet and galloped back toward the barn with Nicole in hot pursuit. They entered the heated tack room to find his mother waiting for them.

"I'll just step outside to let you have some privacy to shift back," she said in what Nicole could only think of as a resigned voice.

Once she had closed the door behind her and they were alone, Asher shifted back.

"All you need to do is ask her to relinquish control and she will," he said quietly. His voice, too, had an oddly tired and resigned tone.

Nicole thanked her she-wolf for an amazing experience and promised her she would not abide by Ellis' edicts. There had been too much joy in running free as a she-wolf with her mate.

"I love you," she said going to him. "We're in this together. He couldn't control you when you were a lone wolf. You are no longer alone."

"I love you," he said kissing her. "This will likely be unpleasant. My mother is going to want you to go with her to our room." He held up his hand to still her argument. "I need you to go with her. This has been coming between me and my sire for a long time. Please, Nicole, just go to our room and wait for me. Can you do that for me?"

"I don't like it, but I can and will. Just remember, we are a bonded pair."

He grinned, leaning down to kiss her. "We are indeed. And before you ask, I will do this out of love for my mother and out of respect for his position as alpha."

"I'm sorry. I shouldn't have asked."

"Of course, you should. It is only natural to want to shift and run with your mate, especially as a newly turned she-wolf. He is old and set in his ways. He cannot see the proverbial forest for the trees and in time the Mystic River Pack will be no more, and Wolf Run will be deserted."

She linked her hand with Asher's, and they joined his mother in the barn.

"He's very angry, Ash. Why?" his mother asked in a concerned voice.

"You know why. If for no other reason than my fated and bonded mate wanted to run free for the first time."

"You cannot take a mate without his blessing," his mother said, softly.

Asher snorted a harsh laugh. "You don't believe that any more than I do, nor does he, for that matter. Nicole is my fated mate and whatever he's been dreaming up was never going to be. You had to know that."

"I hoped," said his mother. "But when I saw you

with Nicole, I knew, and so did he. If you'd just given me a bit of time to bring him around."

"To what, mother? The fact that he and I will never see eye-to-eye, and that I will never live under his iron rule? The only reason I don't challenge him is because of what it would do to you. God knows the pack would be better off."

"Asher, don't say that," his mother pleaded.

"Change of plans, Nicole. We'll head up to the house. I'll let my father know we're heading back to Mystic River. Someone will find us a bed. While I'm doing that and arranging for transportation if he won't loan us a vehicle, can you get us packed?"

Nicole said nothing but nodded and held his hand as they walked back toward the house. She felt as if she understood what a condemned prisoner might feel. No one was going to kill them, but she had the distinct feeling that Asher's relationship with his father wouldn't survive the encounter.

As they entered the door, Gemma tried to say something.

"Don't," said Nicole as she watched Asher head towards his father's study. She looked at Gemma. "There is nothing either of us can do. Your mate chose this course. He doesn't seem to know the first thing about the man he sired. You will always be welcome wherever we are. Ellis? Not so much."

Nicole turned and headed up the stairs to the

room she had shared ever so briefly with her mate. At the top of the stairs, she turned to look down at Gemma, who looked as though her heart was being torn apart.

CHAPTER 18

NICOLE

It didn't take long for her to pack their meager belongings that were at Wolf Run. Grabbing everything she thought they would need, she headed down the stairs with Asher's Navy duffel and their winter coats.

She could hear two raised male voices. They weren't loud enough that you could hear the words, but it was clear that they were angry and coming to a crescendo where one of them, most likely Asher, would simply withdraw from the conflict. There was no way to win with his father. If she knew it after knowing the man less than a day, she was quite certain her mate did.

"Please, Nicole, take those things back upstairs. Talk to Asher," his mother pleaded.

"I'm sorry, Gemma, I can't. This is Ash's decision, and I will live with whatever he decides. You need to understand; Asher isn't alone anymore. Your husband is about to lose his son. If Asher doesn't want him around us, then that's the way it'll be."

The sound of a door being flung open and slamming into the wall was easily heard, as were Asher's heavy footsteps as he strode towards them.

"Come back here, you ungrateful whelp!" roared Ellis.

"We're leaving. He thinks if he doesn't give us a vehicle, we're stuck. I can call…"

Nicole shrugged. "We can shift and find some place to hole up until dawn and we can get back to Mystic River and then down to Kodiak. We don't ever have to come back here again unless you want to. I told your mother she was always welcome to visit."

"You foolish girl," snarled Ellis.

She could feel her hackles rise— not that she had any in human form, but still she could feel that and see her she-wolf growling and ready to pounce. "I'm foolish? You're even more stupid than I thought you were, which says a lot considering how little I thought of you."

"I am your alpha," he bellowed.

"The fuck you are," she snapped back. "I have never been a member of this pack. I've known you less than twenty-four hours and I know I wouldn't want to be a member of any pack that called you alpha. Your son is my alpha and my fated mate."

"That's enough, little wolf," said Asher with a wry

grin. "He knows all of this; he just howls into the wind to hear the sound of his own vanity." He took her hand in his and lifted it to his lips, kissing her fingers. "You are my beloved. No one will ever come between us." He looked over her head to his father. "And I will kill anyone who tries."

He helped her into her coat before putting on his own and kissing his mother's cheek. Gemma was openly weeping.

Nicole went to her. "I'm sorry it had to be like this."

Nicole turned from her; she and Asher walked out into the night. She supposed they could have taken one of the vehicles from Wolf Run, but even the one Asher had driven to the estate belonged to his father, and so they left it where he'd parked it. They were together. They would be fine.

"You must be exhausted," he said wearily. "I'll get hold of Kyra or Jax and get us a ride once we're off Wolf Run."

"I meant what I said."

"I know you did, and that means the world to me, but I would not be worthy of you if after all you've been through, I allowed you to sleep in wolf form to appease my pride."

"It wasn't pride, Ash," she said as their boots crunched through the snow.

"Maybe not all of it, but I'm honest enough with

myself and with you to know that pride, on both of our parts, played into it."

"I feel sorry for your mother. I'll call and check on her tomorrow."

He smiled sadly. "You would have made a great mistress to our pack. I suspect we will receive word that we have been banished."

"He can't banish me from a pack I never belonged to."

He chuckled. "That isn't how it works, but I love you for believing that."

They got to the end of the drive and Nicole was exhausted, but she refused to let Asher know that. He had enough on his mind, and she could feel the heaviness of his heart. Even though they couldn't find common ground, she knew the thought of being banished and never seeing his mother or his home again weighed on him. She vowed to find a way to keep the lines of communication open between Gemma and her son.

The snow, which had stopped falling before they'd gone for their run, began again and was picking up in strength. They came to the gates and Asher punched in the code.

"Here's hoping he hasn't changed it," said Ash.

"That's a shame," said a tall, lean man with angular features as he stepped out of a large, luxury SUV with chains on the tires parked on the opposite side of the gate. "My driver hasn't gotten to hack

Wolf Run's systems in a long time and was looking forward to it."

Asher's face was inscrutable for a moment but changed to a grin as the gates began to slowly swing open. He escorted her through them and extended his hand.

"Colby. I didn't think I'd see you. Nicole, this is Colby Reynolds, what passes for Mystic River's criminal organization. Colby, my fated mate, Nicole."

"The lynx-shifter," she said, a part of her not sure she wanted to shake his hand. There was something dangerous about Colby Reynolds, something not quite right. She couldn't put her finger on it, but Nicole prided herself on her instincts about people.

"I see your mate has made sure you are well informed."

"My mate and I have no secrets."

"I see that," said Reynolds. "I wonder if that's wise. So many secrets are best left buried in the dark."

"Only because they would wither, die, and lose their power if they came out into the light," rejoined Asher. "Get in the SUV, Nicole."

"He didn't invite us…"

"Trust me, Colby didn't drive all the way out here just to piss my father off by driving slowly past the gates, although he did indulge in that kind of thing when he was a kid. He's going to give us a lift to wherever he has arranged for us to stay. He likes people to believe he's a great fixer and that there isn't anything he can't do."

Colby's smile reminded her more of a snake than a lynx. She didn't trust him, but she trusted Asher, and if he wanted her in the nice, warm vehicle, she was going to get in the nice, warm vehicle. It was cold and getting colder all the time.

"Please," said Colby, gesturing to the warm interior. "Although, I'm surprised he'd let a beautiful creature like you interact with predatory cats."

Nicole pulled down the scarf she'd wrapped around her neck to reveal Asher's claiming bite. "Too late, besides I've always preferred large, loving wolves and their ability to knot their mates versus that whole barbed cock thing. That sounds perfectly dreadful."

Asher laughed. "She shoots; she scores. Give it up, Colby. You arguing with my mate is a little like a one-legged man in a butt kicking contest."

"Well, she doesn't lack for spirit," said Colby.

Nicole got into the car, snuggling next to Asher as soon as he was inside.

As the driver started down the icy, deserted road, Colby said, "You have options. The first option is Jax said you could sleep in the jail. Not ideal. The second option is to come to Windsong and stay in the main house."

"A federal employee staying with a gangster…" said Asher.

"Again, not ideal. Your third option is a remote

cottage at the furthest boundary from the manor house. It is outside our perimeter walls but is safe. It's not much, but it has a comfortable bed and a makeshift kitchen. I can have someone bring you groceries and a vehicle tomorrow morning."

Asher looked out the window. "If it keeps snowing like this, you might want to make that a snowmobile."

"The cottage it is. Do you need me to let Jax know where you'll be?"

"I have a sat phone with me."

"How did you know we'd need a lift?" asked Nicole.

"Your mate is as hot tempered as his father. They've never gotten along well, and Ash hasn't been home in years. Add a pretty turned human as a mate without getting his sire and alpha's permission, and I didn't think it would go well. Sometimes he and Jax like to forget there was a time we were all the best of friends, a veritable band of brothers."

"Your choice, not ours," said Ash.

"True enough," responded Colby. "But still, I appreciate you allowing me to assist you. I rather imagine I have Nicole to thank for that."

"Me?" she said, leaning forward before Asher pulled her back against him.

"Yes. Your mate is too proud and too stubborn. He would have shifted and found a hollowed-out tree or a cave of some sort before he took my help. But he has you to think of and I thought he might be willing to bend if he loved you as much as people say."

"How do you know all of this," she asked.

"You'd be surprised with what I know… and how I know it."

Asher shook his head. "Nothing would surprise me about you anymore."

"Time will tell, my old friend. Time will tell."

They drove along the back roads until they could see a comfortable cottage in the distance. There was smoke coming out of the chimney and there were lights in the yard and inside the house.

"Oh, good. They got there in time to get it set up. Don't worry, Nicole, it has all the modern amenities. The fire is just for… well, who doesn't love a crackling fire. But it has both heat and air conditioning, although I think it will be a while before we need the latter. I asked my cook to pack things for breakfast and snacks, and had him send them with my people to set the place up. We'll bring you groceries for however long you have to stay and a snowmobile. Anytime you'd like to take a meal at the house, please know you are always welcome. If you change your mind and would rather be up at the manor, just come up. There's plenty of room."

They arrived in front of an adorable cottage that looked as though it had been picked up in some quaint English village and dropped down on Kodiak Island.

"I've always wondered, how does a thatched roof keep out the weather?" asked Nicole.

"It's synthetic thatch. It really acts as another layer of insulation. Beneath it is a metal roof over a layer of insulation, specifically designed for Alaska, and beneath that a tin ceiling. The windows look charming and authentic, but they are the best insulating windows money can buy. I think you'll be quite pleased with the amenities."

The SUV rolled to a stop and Asher helped her out and into the cottage. Colby was right—it was bright, cheery, and warm. Not as nice as Asher's cabin in the woods but a similar design without bedroom walls.

"Thanks, Colby. I do appreciate both the ride and the accommodations," said Asher, shaking his old friend's hand again.

"My pleasure. Stay as long as you like. I had hoped… oh well, it doesn't really matter what I hoped. I suppose it was never meant to be. We'll leave you to it. There is a landline up to the house. Let us know if you need anything. The cottage is hooked up to our security system, so you should be safe. Besides it's too cold for criminals to be stalking the night." He took Nicole's hand, dropping it when Asher growled. "It was lovely to meet you, Nicole."

"Thank you and thank you for your help."

When Colby and his men had departed, she

turned to Asher. "Okay, that was weird. Do you know why this cottage is here?"

Asher nodded. "Yes, he hoped when his sister and Jax ended their affair that she'd move back to Windsong. He wasn't stupid enough to think she'd live at the manor or even on the estate, but this is the kind of place that would appeal to Kyra. I suspect he offered it to her."

"Your friend Jax had an affair with one of his closest friend's little sister? I'll bet that went over like a lead balloon."

"You might say that. But before you think ill of Jax, they may have been lovers, but it was casual on both their parts. Neither of them was ever in it for the long haul. They were more good friends with benefits. In fact, I doubt they feel any differently now than they did when they were together. They just don't have sex anymore."

"As long as they're both okay with it, it's none of my business. This place is beautiful, but I like our cabin in Kodiak better."

He smiled. "Hey, how did you know about lynx-shifters and their barbs."

Nicole shrugged. "Simple, all felines have barbs along their penises. Maddie Owen doesn't just write about wolves, you know."

"Actually, no, I didn't. Come on, let's go to bed. You've had a fairly eventful day."

Nicole stood at the window, watching the

retreating taillights. She was startled when Asher's sat phone rang. He made a face when he saw the caller ID.

"Jax?" he said, putting it on speaker phone. "I have Nicole with me. She knows everything."

"Not everything. I decided to do a little investigating. What you told me about her buying new climbing cord and knowing what she was doing didn't sit right with me. The rocks on Pyramid aren't normally sharp enough to cut a line like that. So, I went up the mountain myself and found where you found her. I followed the gouges she left with her ice axe. Nice job, Nicole."

"Um, thanks, but we both know I'd be dead if it wasn't for Ash."

"True, but still I know incredibly experienced climbers who wouldn't have been able to self-arrest like that."

"Your point?" asked Ash.

"Right, sorry. Before I get to my point, I did clean up all of the debris you left behind, so you don't need to worry about it."

"Why? It wasn't bothering anyone, and I was going to do it when we could get out of Mystic River. By the way, we're at the cottage at Colby's."

"I know. He just called. I thought I'd let your mom know."

"Thanks, Jax, now why did you clean up where Nicole fell?"

"Because I didn't want anyone to know how she fell or how badly she was hurt."

"She said the cord snapped."

"But it didn't," said Jax.

"Yes, it did," said Nicole. "One minute I was fine and the next I was falling."

"Oh, I have no doubt it was the cord that made you fall. But it wasn't frayed or defective. The damn thing was cut, and by someone who didn't know or didn't care that we'd be able to tell what had been done."

Silence hung in the air until Nicole found a voice to speak. "You mean someone tried to sabotage my climb?"

"No, sweetheart," said Ash gently, wrapping his arm around her. "He means someone tried to kill you."

CHAPTER 19

Nicole had never once, in her entire life, been speechless, but she was now.

"Ash? Are you and Nicole still there?" asked Jax over the phone.

"Yeah, Jax, we are. Nicole is just a bit stunned."

"No. No. I'm fine. Well, okay, I'm not fine but… who the hell would want to kill me? Are you sure?"

"I'm afraid so," said Jax. "As I said, either the person didn't know that we'd be able to tell or didn't care. I have to say that if you'd died, I'm not really sure the clean-up crew would have taken time to look."

"Why did you?" she asked.

"Because you're Asher's mate. But when I got there…"

"How did you get there in these conditions. I hope you didn't put yourself at risk for me."

"Bear-shifter," said Asher, "remember?"

Jax chuckled. "Don't let it rattle you, Nicole. It can take some getting used to, but yes, I shifted and went up the side of the mountain as a bear. Also, Ash had said you were careful and had some experience. To me, that said you'd check your gear."

"Then why didn't I see it?"

"Because it was cut and then glued back together. As long as you weren't putting too much pressure on the cord, it would have been hard to see. When you started to come down and hit the line, it severed and you fell. Lucky for you, it wasn't far, you knew how to use your ice axe, and Asher got to you in time." His tone changed, lightened. "Might I say, you seem awfully cool and collected about this whole shifter thing."

"She reads Maddie Owen," supplied Asher.

Jax groaned.

"They're excellent books and Asher turned me to save my life."

"How are the people we brought in doing?" Asher asked, changing the subject.

"Doc says it looks like everyone is going to be okay. Everybody has been alerted that we have non-shifters in town. The weather should clear, and we should be able to get them out in a day or two."

"That soon?" asked Nicole.

"Colby has a couple of snow buses that can handle the weather and terrain, and we'll start getting them down to Kodiak when we can," said Jax. "Every now and again, he remembers he used to be a good man."

"He still is, Jax. He's just lost his way."

"I suppose he could be worse, but still… I have to live with the fact that he's doing illegal shit right under my nose."

"You could arrest him," said Ash.

"I could, but we both know I'm not going to. For one thing, it would kill Kyra. She has such a hard time reconciling the big brother she knew and loved with the gangster he's become. But as I said to her, at least he keeps the other thugs at bay. What's the cottage like? He built it for Kyra. She said it was pretty."

"She's been here?" asked Nicole.

"She snowshoed in one time just to take a look."

"It is really nice. I like our cabin better."

"Our cabin, is it?" Jax laughed.

"Damn straight it's ours," said Asher. "That bite wasn't just about saving her life. One way or another, she'd have been bearing one."

"You wolves and your damn claiming bites. For the record, Nicole, we bears are much more civilized."

"Civilized?" scoffed Asher. "They have a cere-mony where the shifter slices open your hand with a knife, then does the same to his own. Then they bind the two hands together so that blood is exchanged."

"Ewww!"

"It's much more romantic than the way that wolf of yours makes it sound."

Nicole laughed.

"In any event, I wanted you both to know. Nicole, can you think of anyone who'd want to harm you?" asked Jax.

"Other than Asher's father or my ex, no."

"Ellis?" asked Jax.

"He didn't even know about her before I brought her to Mystic River. She and my father crossed swords. She's a bit overly protective of me," said Asher, giving her a hug.

"Good. He needs protecting where Ellis is concerned. What about your ex?"

"Kevin is all bluster and no follow through. He called me a couple of months ago, wanting money. Saying our townhouse wasn't worth as much, blah, blah, blah. I told him he could kiss my ass and then hung up. He called again while I was up here in Kodiak, and I blew him off."

"Not necessarily your best idea. Have Asher send me the pertinent info—name, address, social security number if you have it, driver's license…"

"I'm telling you, Kevin isn't capable," insisted Nicole.

"Have you ever changed the beneficiaries on any of your insurance policies or bank accounts?" asked Jax.

"I haven't gotten around to it yet…"

"We'll get that done first thing, and I'll be sure Kevin knows it's been done, and that Nicole and I are married."

"Whoa. That was fast. I mean I knew she was your fated mate, but still."

"But still nothing. If she wants a big fancy wedding, she can have one after this mess is over with, but as soon as we can get Judge Freeman to do the deed, we'll get it done."

"Don't I get a say in that?"

"No," was the collective answer from Jax and Asher.

"You two take care of each other and I'll let Judge Freeman know, which means the whole town is going to know." Both men laughed. "I'm sure I don't have to tell you but keep her close, Asher. That fall was no accident."

"Will do, and thanks, Jax."

Asher ended the call.

"It's not Kevin. Don't get me wrong, he's sleazy enough and might even be desperate enough. But he's a huge fan of police procedurals. He'd know about you being able to tell if the rope was cut and not frayed or severed by a rock."

"Maybe, but desperate men don't always make the best choices. Jax is right, it's not unheard of for someone to not question a fall. Climbing is inherently dangerous and even the best climbers can make one little mistake and have it cost them their lives."

"You would have," she said. "Even if we hadn't become involved or even met. You would have looked to make sure so you could give peace and closure to the person's survivors and justice to the one who died."

"I'm not a romantic hero from one of Maddie Owen's books."

"No. You're my romantic hero, and I don't have to share you with all of her other readers. I knew I was falling for you long before you tore a chunk out of my neck."

He chuckled. "Duly noted. You should know I'm torn between wanting to spank your sexy ass for challenging a male alpha wolf, being so proud of your courage for doing so, and being humbled that you love me so much that you would."

"Let's go for options two or three."

Asher laughed. "This time. Do it again, and only option one will be available."

"Understood."

"Until we find out who is responsible, I don't want you off by yourself. You stick close to me, Jax, or Kyra."

"You're really spooked by Jax's theory, aren't you?"

"Aren't you? If not, you should be. Trust me, if

Jax said somebody cut that rope, they cut the rope. The only reason to cut somebody's climbing cord is to get them killed or badly injured. In either event, I want you safe." Nicole shivered. "Are you all right?"

"I guess it hadn't really hit me what you and Jax were saying. I almost wish I did think it was Kevin, but I can't believe it's him. Not having a clue as to who could hate me that much is almost more frightening."

"It'll be all right, Nicole. I'll keep you safe, and we'll figure it out."

❧

Asher

Asher checked the door and windows to make sure they were secure and that the alarm was working. While he was getting things locked up, Nicole turned the bed back, removed her clothes, and crawled into bed.

"You look exhausted. I shouldn't have taken you for a run," he said softly as he sat on the edge of the mattress and removed his own clothes.

"Yeah, you should have. I loved it. It was as if I could feel what she feels…"

"You can. It isn't as if you lose consciousness; you just experience everything in a different way. You retain all of the memories of what happened when you shifted to wolf." He drew back the covers on his side of the bed. "You aren't tired?"

Nicole wriggled onto her back and spread her legs in blatant invitation. "For you? Never."

"Careful mate, I may hold you to that."

He joined her in the bed, spreading her legs further apart and moving down her body, whispering kisses as he went. When he reached her sex, he hovered his mouth just over her labia, inhaling deeply and smiling.

"God, you smell good."

Asher settled his mouth on her and gave the swollen nub at the apex of her thighs a gentle lick, before latching on and sucking hard. Nicole's hips surged up and he could feel the heat rolling off her. Her arousal was sharp and tangy, and he moved down to make a meal of her pussy. He speared her core with his tongue again and again, feasting on the wealth of honey he found there. Nothing had ever tasted better than Nicole's arousal.

Her hips began undulating and her breathing indicated she was close. She'd needed this as much as he did. He focused on bringing her pleasure, moving one hand up to play with her nipples as the other fingers of the other hand played gently with her clit.

Far more quickly than he'd expected, her body stiffened as she thrust her pussy into his face, calling his name as she came, her entire body trembling before she sighed and went limp in his hands.

He rocked back onto his knees. "You are so beautiful."

"You make me feel that way."

He crawled up her body, dragging himself along her sensitized skin before settling and making a place for himself. He dragged his cock over her clit, moving it gently between pussy and nub and back again, coating it with the residue of her orgasm.

They were safe. If he could trust Colby with nothing else, Asher knew he could trust him with that. He had no doubt the wily lynx-shifter knew what Jax had found. He could feel the base of his cock swelling as the alpha knot began to form. He watched Nicole's face and knew she was lost to her own revelry.

Positioning his cock at her core, he said, "I love you, Nicole."

He thrust up hard, driving the alpha knot past her resisting entrance, causing her to cry out. Nicole's body shook as she pushed at him, trying to dislodge him. Asher growled deep within his throat before capturing her mouth in a brutally passionate kiss. He continued to kiss her, tangling their tongues together and emitting a low resonant call to which Nicole instinctively responded.

"Easy love," he murmured, nuzzling her neck and forcing himself to remain still, allowing her body to accept and accommodate the invasion that only a male alpha wolf could give to his mate.

He lessened the dominance of his kisses, allowing

seduction to come to the forefront. When her body began to soften and she began to return his kisses, he knew she was beginning to experience the intimacy and sensuality of the knot. Nicole was passionate and responsive; Asher had no doubt she would learn to crave his knot buried deep inside her.

"Shit, Asher. That hurt. I wasn't expecting that."

"I know, but I needed to possess you completely and I worried if we talked about it, you'd be tense and make it worse."

"I don't think you quite understand how painful that is."

"I do, but I promise what comes now will more than make up for it."

He hissed in pain as the knot began to swell further. It was a phenomenon of the knot that while it was uncomfortable as it formed, once it breached the entrance to a she-wolf's core, the final swelling to seal her to him was incredibly painful. He nuzzled her neck and held her close until she ceased to struggle against him and instead wrapped herself around him, binding herself as closely to him as he was to her. Nicole nuzzled the hollow of his throat as he stroked her skin, whispering words of encouragement, praise, and sex.

Her response was everything he could have hoped for and then some. He slid his hands down her body and beneath her so he could hold her in place as he began to rock his hips forward and back, the alpha knot allowing him to only move in short, deep thrusts. Her pussy spasmed along his length, including the knot, in a way that produced an ecstasy that was incomparable to any other.

Nicole cried out as she came in a powerful orgasm, clawing at his back and urging him on. She arched up into his body, her eyes rolling back in her head as she surrendered to him, the knot, and the destiny that lay before them. He continued to rock with her, glorying in the pleasure she gave him and that which he gave in return.

Nicole began to climax repeatedly, one coming right after another, the frenzy of his abbreviated thrusting increasing until he was pounding into her like a man possessed. He could feel the tingling at the base of his spine as he rocked her even more aggressively. He could feel his cum as it began to rush up from his balls, through the knot, and down his shaft. His seed gushed into her, bathing what he knew would be her sore pussy. She arched her body, molding it to his as her pussy tightened around him, pulsing to milk his cock dry. Finally, when he had emptied himself completely within her, he settled himself and rolled to his back, taking her with him.

He stroked her fevered body, allowing her to come back to him in her own time. She purred in contentment, and he rumbled to her soothingly, urging her to sleep. Nicole nestled into his body, finding a place she felt comfortable and secure, and fell asleep, locked in his embrace by the still swollen alpha knot.

It was a long time before Asher could do the same. Someone had tried to kill her. He needed to find out who and stop whoever it was before they had a chance to finish the job.

CHAPTER 20

NICOLE

When she finally woke the next morning, it wasn't to another round of sex with Asher, which with or without the knot, wasn't a bad way to wake up. Instead, it was to the sound of a closing door and the aroma of bacon and some kind of doughy thing with yeast and cinnamon.

She sat up in bed, trying not to wince. Being knotted and tied to Asher had been amazing, but it had also made her sore. And surprisingly, while it wasn't something she had expected to ever want to do again, she found she couldn't wait for the next round.

"Whatever that is," she said as Asher walked toward the bed, tray in hand, "I want some."

Asher chuckled. "I figured you'd be hungry. There wasn't a lot here that lent itself to making a good breakfast quickly. I decided to take Colby at his word and called up to see if they could bring us down something to tide us over until we could get something more substantial ready." He sat down on the edge of the bed and set the tray down on the bedside table, leaning down to give her a deep kiss. "Good morning, my beautiful mate."

She could feel lust, love, joy, concern, and contentment all jumbled together and rolling down the bonding link that existed between fated mates.

She wrapped her arms around his strong neck. "Last night was incredible."

"That is the way of most fated mates. They feel everything more deeply and are far more connected to each other."

"I always thought that instant connection and love at first sight were just made-up plot devices for romance writers." She smiled at her own foolishness. "Curiously, I found it easy to believe in wolf-shifters and knots, but not the emotion behind it."

"Hmm... that says something about your upbringing. Wolves are almost indoctrinated from birth to believe there is one being who can complete them and that without him or her, we are condemned to live a half-life. I had almost begun to believe that was the hand fate had dealt me. And then you walked into my life, wanting to make a solo climb in my backyard."

"And almost got myself killed. You and Randy were right; I shouldn't have tried it."

"No, we were wrong. You were ready, judging by

everything I've seen. Someone tried to kill you. They sabotaged your climbing cord to do it. By the time the storm started, you would have been off the technical part of the mountain. Depending on your driving skill in bad weather, you should have made it safely back to your hotel."

Wrapping her hands around the coffee mug, Nicole leaned back. "For what it's worth, I had planned to call from my rental vehicle to gauge how angry you were."

"And if I'd told you that you could expect to be put over my knee?" he asked, pulling off a piece of the cinnamon roll and feeding it to her.

"Mmm, that's delicious. I'd have probably come, anyway. I've never been spanked before. I don't know that I'd say I liked it…"

"If you had, I would think I'd done it wrong," he chortled.

"Then why did the pain turn me on?"

"It didn't, although you do like your pleasure with a bit of bite to it. Pun intended. I think for you it's more about having someone to whom you're accountable and who can allow you to find respite from the rest of your world."

She nodded. "You could be right about that. I love my job as an event planner and having Judith trust me to open the Seattle office was a huge boost to my self-confidence, which after the disastrous end of my marriage, I badly needed. Of course, I also give some credit for that to the staff at *Lobo Bahía*."

"*Lobo Bahía*? The Steele's hotel in San Francisco?"

"Yes. Do you know it? I kind of thought it was the best kept secret boutique hotel in San Francisco."

Asher laughed. "Obviously you don't know the Steele brothers—Linc and Damian."

"I met Linc once while I was staying there."

"Linc and Damian Steele are wolf-shifters. The hotel's name literally translates to Wolf Bay."

"No shit?" she said excitedly. "Are they friends of yours?"

"Not close friends but I know both of them. Damian is technically the alpha of the pack, but he and his brother are close and so Linc is basically the alpha of San Francisco even though the city is part of Damian's territory."

"Is Grace Steele…"

"A turned human, like you."

Nicole threw back her head and laughed. "She must think I'm a gullible idiot. I saw the mark on her neck and commented that it reminded me of something I'd read about in a book. She said people said that to her all the time."

"If we go down to San Francisco, we can go to her restaurant and you can show her yours," he said popping the last piece of cinnamon roll into her mouth.

"So there really are wolf-shifters all over, even in Seattle?"

"Even in Gig Harbor. That is the territory of Daniel Lawson."

"The vintner? Oh my god, of Wolf Song Vineyard?"

He grinned. "One and the same."

"I'm beginning to think you're right, that we were inevitable."

"Of course, I am. Think about it, what compelled you to try Pyramid Mountain for your solo climb? There are a lot of mountains that are an easier climb closer to you."

"I guess part of it was that it was here on Kodiak and seemed more adventurous than something closer to home. Besides, I was coming up here anyway for business. Speaking of which, do you think Mystic River might want to become a destination wedding venue? The town seems so picturesque, and it could mean additional income."

"They might. I'd talk to Jax and some of the vendors you'd want to use. We don't discourage humans who want to use it as a base. We just make sure everyone in town knows, especially those like wolves, that are not common or not at all known here on Kodiak. If that were to happen and someone caught them in their altered state it would raise a lot of questions."

"Then I'll start with Jax and Scott and work my way outward."

"Do you think the company you work for might open an office here on Kodiak?"

"I've thought about that, and I don't know that Alaska would generate enough business," she said, as they sat down and began to eat.

"What aren't you telling me? I can feel something. It's more than just leaving a job that you love."

"Yes. When I got divorced, Judith was having cash flow issues and knew that I would have cash to invest so she offered me a deal. I would come up and open the Seattle Office. The agreement was that once we were in the black, I'd become a full partner with a sixty/forty split and that in four years, which is coming up, it would be fifty-one/forty-nine. We've been wildly successful so that additional nine percent would be substantial. There is a non-compete clause, but Alaska lies outside of the restriction."

"Would you get your investment paid back?"

"I've made that back and more." She leaned toward him and kissed him lightly. "You're worth far more to me than money. Our life is here. I'll just open my own business and base it out of Kodiak. This island is so gorgeous and for a lot of people, especially those in the Pacific Northwest that want a more rustic wedding venue, Alaska is perfect."

"So, I don't have to feel guilty about making you leave a job you've put your heart into."

"I think we both know that my heart belonged to you from the day you brought me back from death."

"I gave you mine, as well. We'll make a good life here. We may not have a pack..."

"We'll start our own. Maybe give those of the Mystic River Pack an alternative to leaving the island."

"That isn't the worst idea. There are plenty of wolves, especially the younger ones, who wouldn't mind having a choice. But I want to figure out who tried to kill you and why."

"I think once we know the answer to one, we'll know the answer to the other."

"Agreed. You're sure it's not your ex?"

"Kevin wanted money and Jax is right, I haven't changed my beneficiaries, which I will get done. It's not that I think that he isn't capable of murdering me for money. The new soon-to-be-ex-wife is using my divorce attorney, so he is hard-up for cash, but if Jax could tell the rope had been tampered with, it wasn't him."

"But then who? Could it be the soon-to-be-ex?"

"How would she benefit from my death?"

Asher shrugged as he cleared the small table. "If your money and any insurance proceeds revert to Kevin, there's more money for her."

Nicole nodded slowly, joining him in the kitchen and pushing him aside to do the dishes. "You cooked, let me clean up."

"You are supposed to be taking it easy, remember? Shifting to go for a run and my knotting and tying you aside."

"We'll split the difference. You wash, I'll dry. I suppose you could be right about Kevin's soon-to-be-ex, but how did she get to it? She would have had to have access to it. I don't even know if she knows I've taken up climbing. For that matter, neither does Kevin."

"You're right. Whoever sabotaged your climbing cord had to have access, and I'm assuming you and your ex weren't chummy."

"That would be a correct assumption. Besides, both of them live in San Francisco."

"Any chance you pissed off someone here in Alaska?"

"Other than your father?" she teased.

"Don't think I didn't consider that, but he had no real motive and didn't even know you. Besides, I doubt he had access to your climbing gear before the accident that wasn't really an accident."

"How come Jax wants to keep the fact that someone tried to hurt me?"

"Kill you. I doubt very much they thought you'd survive. They had no idea how good a climber you are."

"Okay, but why doesn't Jax want people to know?"

"My guess is, he'd like it if whoever it was showed his or her hand."

"Any chance we're looking for a rival for your affection?"

"Mine? Good god, no. I am the lone wolf, remember? And until you came along, I kept my private life private."

"I find it hard to believe that you were celibate."

"No, but I don't think it's a good idea for someone in a position of perceived power to be sleeping around in his own backyard. There are places in Anchorage and Fairbanks where a shifter can find what he needs, but its consensual and there's an agreement in place."

"You mean like a sex club? This just gets better and better," she said, gleefully.

Asher rolled his eyes and groaned. "Don't start; besides, for that to be the case, they'd have had to know we'd become an item and sabotaged your gear the one night we were together."

"So, if it didn't happen here… and you're right that whoever it was, if it was up here, would have only had the one night. Would the glue or whatever they used to put it back together even have time to set up?"

"Good point. So, for the sake of the argument, let's assume it didn't happen here in Alaska. Any competitors in Seattle that see you as a threat to their business?"

"Plenty," she laughed. "We've been touted as one of the fastest growing businesses in the country. Not just event planning, but overall. My investment in the company Judith started has been a major boon for me. I've made back my initial investment at least ten times over, and had I been staying, I would have become incredibly wealthy. I'm sure Judith saw it as a shrewd business maneuver on her part, and some of my friends saw it as her taking advantage. The thing is, I saw it as a tremendous opportunity and jumped on it."

He stopped drying the last dish. "Are you sure you want to walk away from that?"

"I don't see it as walking away from anything. I see it as walking toward my own happily ever after. As I said, I've more than made back my initial investment and I learned so much both about the scope of event planning and starting a business. Because I had Judith to lean on, I didn't make a lot of common mistakes first-time entrepreneurs do. I also learned to look at unique experiences for our clients and partnering with locals."

"Sounds like your business will be a benefit to the island."

"I was surprised that there didn't seem to be an event planning company here on Kodiak. There's the convention center and a couple of guide outfits, but really no one who does what I do. There are places on the mainland, but I'll bet they don't really make exclusive use of the island and all of the artisans and places. Someone here with 'boots on the ground' I think will have an advantage."

"Agreed. The fact that you're a local, that you chose to leave the lower forty-eight to be with the one you love and make a life here will make a difference. Hell, maybe you should start a matchmaking service for shifters," he added with a laugh.

"Could that work? I mean can shifters be made into other shifters or is only human DNA subject to change?"

"They can; it's frowned upon, but then, so is taking a human mate in some groups."

"Do they form a hybrid of some kind?"

"No; the stronger DNA overwhelms the other. It is far more dangerous and as many people die from trying as are successful."

"So, could a mixed species couple have kids?"

"Looking to take Colby up on his offer?"

"No, thanks. Your knot was amazing, but a barbed penis? Not so much."

He laughed and they finished up and got ready for the day. Asher was adamant that even with the cottage being covered by Colby's security system, he didn't want Nicole left by herself. He was convinced, as was Jax, that if and when whoever had tried to kill her found out she had survived, they would try again.

Nicole wasn't sure she agreed with them, but she also wasn't in a hurry to put it to a test.

CHAPTER 21

NICOLE

*A*sher dropped her by the clinic where Nicole and her offer of help were greeted with open arms. Just as she was running out of charts to create and file, Jax stopped by to let her know he'd drafted Asher to check in with outlying residents to ensure everyone was safe.

"Ash tells me you plan weddings and big corporate events and such."

"Yes. Did he also tell you I think Mystic River would make a wonderful location for some of them?"

"He did, and I'm inclined to agree with you. There are those who might not like the idea of a lot of humans being around, though."

"I can understand that. It's a fear for most small towns with lots of character, but it can be managed. I thought if there was a town council, I'd get on their schedule to make a presentation." .

"There is, and I'll see that you get to do that. I'd also talk to Scott and Trudy."

"Scott owns the bakery, right? And as I recall, does some catering. But who's Trudy?"

"She owns the B and B. It's really the only place for people to stay. She'd like to expand her business and I would think that might be a way for her to do that."

Nicole wrote down her name. "Thanks, Jax."

"No. Thank you."

"I haven't done anything yet."

"Not true. I've known Asher most of my life. I have never known him to be this happy and content. Finding you and knowing you feel the same has done a lot for him. And there isn't one person in town, save the visitors, who doesn't know how you pitched in when you'd just come through a transition. Betty and Doc have sung your praises to anyone within earshot. That says a lot about you. The fact that you're Asher's fated mate is just an added bonus."

"Can I ask what the deal is between you, Asher, and Colby Reynolds?"

"You can ask, but I won't tell you. Neither will Colby. Only Asher can choose to share that with you." It looked as if the sheriff was worried he'd said too much. "Well, I need to get back to the office."

"Sure. Thanks, Jax."

The door closed and Betty stuck her head out. "I'm sure Ash will tell you in time."

"Do you know?"

"I don't even have a clue. I also know that Kyra doesn't know and if anyone should outside the three of them, it's her. She and Jax were an item a few years back and she's Colby's kid sister. I know what everybody says about him, and I have no doubt it's true. He was always in trouble as a kid, but there are times when I see him watching Kyra and I can see his pain. Whatever happened over there needs to get resolved."

"I'll see if I can't move that along."

"I'm sorry you and Ash's father got into it. Ellis can be a real jackass where his son is concerned."

"Gemma says they're too much alike."

"In some ways, but Asher has seen more of the world and is a lot more tolerant." Betty turned to head into the back but stopped at the door. "By the way, a lady stopped in here earlier looking for you."

"What lady?"

"I don't know, and she didn't give a name. I'm not sure what she was doing here. I don't think she was on the train, but then again, if she wasn't, how did she get here and why?"

"That's kind of weird, what did she look like?"

"Tall, reed-thin. Severe straight hair. Looked rich."

"Silver hair? Expensive clothing, as in right off the latest designer runway for outer wear?"

"Yes. Beautiful color. Do you know her?"

"It sounds like Judith Masters, my boss."

"Why would she be here looking for you?"

"I haven't a clue, except maybe she's worried about me. Asher spoke with her and let her know I had a fall and would be staying up here until I was fully recovered."

"You're going back? I thought you were staying with Asher."

"Oh, I am. I'm afraid none of you are getting rid of me."

"Best news of the day," said Betty. "Everybody loves Ash and it's obvious how he feels about you."

"Asher said Colby had some snow buses and was going to start moving people."

Betty nodded. "There's a couple of people we've set up here that Doc doesn't want moved until they're further along in their recovery, but they think they can get the majority moved down to Kodiak by tomorrow at the latest."

"If it's okay with you, I'll go see if I can find Judith. If it wasn't her, I don't know who it was."

"Why don't you just call around and stay here where it's warm?"

Nicole stood up and grabbed her coat. "I'll be fine. I'll just check in a couple of places. Judith is fairly hard to miss or forget."

"She wasn't overly friendly."

"She is when you get to know her, but Alaska during a blizzard has to be her idea of the seventh ring of hell."

Betty laughed and Nicole headed out the door. It was damn cold, and she was thankful that whoever had picked out her clothes and cold-weather gear had known what they were doing. The sidewalks had been cleared and some kind of coating put down that not only kept them from icing back over, but actually seemed to provide some traction.

Interestingly the streets hadn't been plowed, but she could see why—people were using snowmobiles, snowshoes, and horse drawn sleighs to get around town. It might be inconvenient to those who weren't used to it, but it did have a lovely rustic charm—at least the snowshoes and sleighs did.

Mystic River was all that a small town was supposed to be. People waved and called to her by name. She didn't know any of them, but they seemed to know her. News traveled fast. Her first stop was Scott Hardaway's bakery, which smelled divine.

"Hey, you," he called as a greeting, ringing up a customer. "Can I get you some coffee and a ham and cheese croissant?"

"Yum and yes," she replied taking a small table at the front. When he brought the food, she asked him to join her for a few minutes.

"What's up? Should you be out in this cold?"

"I'm fine. I'm sure you know Asher and I are going to get married." The wattage behind Scott's grin could have lit up the holiday tree at Rockefeller Center. "I'm going to start an event planning company and base it out of Kodiak. I'd like to include you in my planning."

"I'm all ears."

"What do you think about using Mystic River as a destination venue?"

"I think it would be a great way for the town and people in it to generate some new revenue streams and any concerns could be managed. I think Trudy will want to talk to you. I know she's been wanting to expand her business but was worried about generating enough new income to justify the expense. And it wouldn't just have to be weddings…"

Nicole nodded. "That's what I was thinking—hunting and fishing trips, corporate retreats, reunions."

"Colby has some undeveloped land adjacent to his compound. He might see an advantage to building small, rustic cabins and a meeting facility. I know Kodiak has a convention center, but something smaller and more intimate might appeal to folks."

"Exactly. Asher said a lot of people get here by boat. Maybe someone would like to come up with a business that does that. In any event, I think it could be a really good thing. I'm glad you like the idea. I wanted to talk to Trudy and see what she thought. Maybe I'll talk to Colby, as well. I spoke with Jax about getting on the agenda for a town meeting and giving a presentation."

"Good idea. I know Trudy will be on board. We

can be there to lend our support, but I don't think you'll have a lot of opposition. A lot of the various shifter groups are losing the younger people as they don't see any opportunities for them."

"The other thing is that every single thing I've had that you made has been delicious. I don't just mean good; I mean certifiably amazing. If I do this, regardless of using Mystic River as a destination venue, would you be willing to come on board as my exclusive caterer? You don't have to ans…"

"Yes. I'm in with both feet."

"That's great. Knowing that means I know what kind of space to look for in Kodiak."

"If you get something with a commercial kitchen, that could handle a lot of the logistics."

"My thought exactly."

"I hope you don't take this the wrong way, but I'm really glad you fell off Pyramid Mountain."

Nicole laughed and realized that Jax really had managed to keep a lid on the fact that someone had meant for her to die on that mountain. It was a sobering thought.

She headed out and took Scott up on his offer to use his snowmobile. When she spoke with Trudy, she received the same enthusiastic response and was excited to hear Scott was all in. Feeling like she had two of the major components of her plan in place, she headed back into town toward the sheriff's office. She had passed the bakery when she was sure she spotted the woman Betty had described. Nicole couldn't see her face well enough to know if it was Judith, but the build, clothing and what she could see of the hair hanging from under the ski hat looked right.

The woman mounted a snowmobile and headed out of town. Nicole didn't think twice about following her. The woman stayed on the road with Nicole following her. When she veered off into the woods, Nicole thought about turning around, but now was incredibly curious. Finally, the woman stopped beside a gazebo that overlooked the river that even in the freezing temperatures ran fast and deep enough to keep flowing.

Nicole parked her snowmobile next to the woman's, dismounted and walked in. The woman had been facing toward the river with her back turned to the entrance. As Nicole entered, she turned and Nicole saw that it was, indeed, Judith. What the hell was she doing here?

Judith shook her head slowly, scowling as she did so.

"Judith? I didn't expect to see you. Didn't Asher give you his sat phone number? I know he let you know I was recovering."

"Yes, he did. He has a very sexy voice. Is he as hunky as he sounds over the phone?"

"He is. I wanted to talk to you, but I was planning to come down to San Francisco."

"Were you? And what did you plan to tell me?"

There was something off about Judith—the way she was standing, the look on her face, the way she was speaking and something cold and dead behind her eyes. She seemed angry, resigned, and a little resentful.

"Judith, are you alright? What are you doing here?"

"I needed to see for myself."

"See what?"

"That you'd lived." Her tone was a mixture of venom and ice. "Why the fuck couldn't you have just died?"

CHAPTER 22

NICOLE

Nicole was taken aback. She couldn't possibly have heard Judith say what she thought she'd heard her say.

"Excuse me?" Nicole said in disbelief.

"You heard me. Why didn't you just die like a good girl? You've always been such a good girl," she said in a derisive tone. "Your death would have been the perfect tragedy. Everyone would have mourned your loss and I could have been your grieving partner and friend. But no, you had to somehow survive a fall off a mountain. How the fuck did you manage that?"

"You?" The complete truth of what she was saying hit Nicole, making her feel as though she'd been body slammed by a truck. "You tried to kill me?" she asked, shaken to her core.

"Yes, and it was the perfect plan. I would have been in San Francisco, and you would have died a noble death following your dream to climb a mountain all by yourself. I'd been trying to come up with the perfect plan for over a year, and then you announced you wanted to come up to some godforsaken wilderness. What a pain in the ass to get here." She shook her head. "When you announced your little plan, I realized I had the opportunity of a lifetime."

"But how? You never had access to my climbing gear."

"Think not? You were so proud of the way you'd found an eco-friendly way to commute from that little harbor town you call home. You gave me a key to your place just for emergencies. I didn't even have to ask for it or figure out a way to get in. I just flew into Sea-Tac and rented a car. It was a major pain in the ass to find someone willing to take cash and not use any ID. Then I drove out to that podunk town and cut your rope. It took for fucking ever for the damn glue to set up. Then I flew home. There is a record of my buying a ticket, but I can just say I flew up for a meeting."

Nicole stumbled back and leaned against the railing. "Why?"

"Does it really matter?"

"It does to me. I thought we were friends."

"We were. Only I hadn't expected you to be as entrepreneurial as you turned out to be. I honestly didn't think the Seattle office would ever make it out of the red. You were supposed to be a tax write off and an influx of cash. Paying you forty percent of my profits…"

Something about that snapped Nicole out of her semi-stupor. "They were my profits, too. I worked hard to make the Seattle office succeed. Damn hard and sank a hell of a lot of my money into it to do so."

"But it never matched what we made in San Francisco. I checked with Poppy. I should have made the agreement read split of the profits on the Seattle office only. Not only did she say she didn't think I could win that argument in court; she said she wouldn't represent me. She didn't feel it would be ethically correct." She said the last two words using air quotes.

"I don't know that I would have been willing to sink every dime I had for just a cut of the Seattle office. After all, a substantial amount of that money went into the San Francisco office. So, you wanted to kill me for the money?" It was obvious, but it seemed a bit overly dramatic even for Judith.

"Why else? I've given everything to my business, and now my cheating spouse thinks he and his baby mama are entitled to half of what's mine, which would mean you'd be making more money than me. Now does that seem fair to you?"

Nicole nodded. "Yes. I'm not the one who keeps marrying fortune hunters. I certainly shouldn't have to pay for your bad choices."

"Well, you won't. The polo player, according to

Poppy, will be limited by the pre-nup and only to what was mine as part of the marriage. In other words, he won't be able to touch what was once yours. So, you see," she said with a nonchalant shrug, "it was the only way for me to come out on top. I don't suppose you'd like to accommodate me and just jump into that river. If the fall from this height didn't kill you, the water certainly would."

"No one who knows me would believe I committed suicide."

"Oh they would once they talked to me back in Seattle."

"Judith, people here in Mystic River have seen you, and Betty knows I think the woman she talked to is you. Sheriff Miller won't buy it for an instant; nor will Ash. You don't really think you can murder me, do you?"

"I do. What I don't think is that some park ranger or a small-town sheriff can do much about it. You'll be dead, and even if somehow they managed to get me arrested, I'll have the best lawyers money can buy." She cackled. "Your money can buy. There's a kind of poetic irony I like about that."

"If I won't jump, just how do you plan to kill me?"

Judith's answer was to pull out a small derringer-type of gun. "I don't think that'll be too much of an issue."

Clearly, Judith had become unhinged, but in a cold, calculating way. She needed to keep her talking to give Asher enough time to realize she was missing from town and find her. Every minute she could keep Judith talking was that much longer for Ash to figure out she hadn't remained in town and that something had gone wrong. She hadn't thought that she was in danger up here in Mystic River. She had been wrong. Once again she had disregarded his concerns and had, however unwittingly, put her life in very real danger.

The fact was, if Judith killed her, it wouldn't matter who was right or wrong. All that would matter was she was dead. She had to keep Judith talking… had to ensure she stayed alive. They say when you are about to die, your life flashes before you. It wasn't true for her. She was staring death in the face, and all she could see was the life she could have with Asher if only she managed to survive long enough for Ash to save her.

"Won't shooting me put a damper on your suicide theory? How will you explain that away? I can tell you for a fact, if you get close enough for there to be stippling on my skin…"

"What the fuck is stippling?"

"Really, Judith, if you're going to go around murdering people you really ought to watch more police procedurals. Stippling, which is also sometimes called tattooing, occurs when some of the residue from the gunshot is left on the victim's skin."

"I'll just wipe the area clean."

"No, see this is where those police procedurals come in handy. The gunpowder residue is forced into the skin and cannot just be wiped off. Stippling would have to happen if I committed suicide with your little gun there."

"I'll shoot you in the heart—through your clothing."

"First, killing me with a shot to the heart isn't as easy as you might think, also suicides don't normally point a gun into their body and fire. They almost always use a head shot either to the temple or through the mouth or from under the chin. And to do that with your cute toy gun, you'll need to be close enough to me that I have a fighting chance at wrestling the gun away from you and turning it on you instead."

"That won't do you any good," said Judith, glancing around. "It'll be your word against mine. You just woke up from a traumatic incident. They'll think you made it up or are being paranoid. I'm very good at playing the innocent victim."

"That's not going to work. I turned on my cell phone's recording app here in my pocket. I've recorded everything. They'll hear you in your own words."

Nicole hadn't done that. She didn't even know if her phone could do that, but Judith sure as hell didn't know.

She needed to keep talking, needed to keep Judith a bit off balance so that she could give Asher time to realize she wasn't in town and come and find her. He would be pissed, but provided she survived, she could live with that. The operative word being *survive*.

"God, you're a pain in my ass. My plan was so good, almost foolproof, and you fucked it all up by not dying."

She was running out of things to say. Time, she needed more time.

Judith raised the gun and aimed it at Nicole. A split second before Judith could pull the trigger or Nicole could leap out of the way, she heard the quiet sound of something large crunching through the ice-covered snow. A loud growl and an enormous wolf jumped through the gazebo's open sides. It landed and then leapt again, straight at Judith, grasping at her wrist with the hand that held the gun, shaking its head viciously until Judith was forced to drop it.

The wolf continued to hold Judith's wrist, and she screamed just as Nicole heard the bones crunch. Judith tried beating and kicking at the wolf, but he would not relinquish his hold. Nicole's heart nearly stopped beating when Judith began to hit and punch at the wolf, who Nicole knew to be Asher.

"Get it off me! Get it off," Judith cried out as she slid to the floor.

Finally, the wolf released its hold, backing away from Judith toward Nicole, growling the entire time, to take a protective stance in front of her. Sirens wafted across the snowy terrain followed by the sound of snowmobiles.

"It's over, Judith. I'm sure that's the sheriff. You're done."

"Damn you," Judith said as she reached out with her other hand to snatch up the gun as it lay on the floor of the gazebo. She stood, grasping the elaborate railing for support. "Why couldn't you just die? Maybe I can tell them that I was trying to kill the wolf when it threatened you and missed, hitting you and then shooting it, as well. Yes, that should work."

The wolf bounded at her, leaping and knocking her and itself over the railing.

"No!" screamed Nicole as she rushed across the gazebo and peered down the ravine to the icy river below just in time to see them both hit the rushing water.

"Nicole!" shouted Jax as he charged in, gun drawn.

She charged past him toward the snowmobile. "It was Judith, my boss. She's the one. Asher attacked her. They both went over the side; we have to get to him."

"You ride with me," growled Jax. "There's a place we may be able to fish them out downstream. Ash may be able to survive the fall and time in the water. I doubt your boss can." Nicole took her place behind him.

"I don't give a damn about Judith. We have to save Ash."

"Hang on!" he called over the sound of the motor as he and Kyra drove the snowmobiles at breakneck speed over the uneven ground.

The wind whipped past Nicole, stinging her face, as they rushed along a diagonal path that was forward, but toward the river as well. At first, Nicole was terrified, not just for Asher's life but her own. She didn't give a second thought to Judith, whose actions had brought about her own end. She realized as they raced towards a destination that only Jax and Kyra seemed to know, that Jax was in complete and total control of the snowmobile and himself.

They arrived at a rickety old bridge that seemed better suited for picturesque photos than for actually crossing the river. Jax turned the snowmobile and hit the brake, causing the machine to fishtail and skid to a halt. Kyra did the same, spraying Nicole and Jax with snow.

"You two wait here. We bears are more suited to cold water. Get blankets and clothing ready for me and Ash."

The sheriff shook himself and then was surrounded by the earth shaking, flames, and an explosion.

Kyra touched her arm. "It's okay. That's how Kodiak shift."

"Amazing," Nicole said.

When the flames died away, Jax had become his Kodiak self. Nicole knew that Kodiak were one of the largest species of bear—some said it was the polar bear, and others the Kodiak. It didn't really matter as Nicole suspected Jax was bigger than any bear the experts had studied.

Jax lumbered down the bank and stepped out into the river, traversing it until he was in the middle. Kyra and Nicole fished through the snowmobiles and got out clothing, towels, and blankets. They rushed to the bank of the river trying to see if they could spot either Judith or Asher. Jax had been right—both of them were headed straight for him. He batted Judith's lifeless body to the edge of the river where Nicole and Kyra grabbed her sodden clothing and pulled her up onto the bank. Jax grabbed Ash in his massive jaws by the scruff of his neck and made his way out of the river.

"I'll check her for life signs; you help Jax and Ash," said Kyra.

"Thank you," Nicole said, giving her a brief hug before following Jax up the hill.

Nicole wrapped a thermal blanket around Asher. Jax snuffled his nose against her hand before retreating to give them some space. Asher was shivering but he was alive. As he huddled in the blanket, Nicole rubbed his luxurious fur to get him as dry as possible.

"If you felt half as helpless and terrified as I am right now when you found me, I am so, so sorry for attempting my solo climb."

Asher raised his head and shook it, before laying it on her shoulder and nuzzling her neck. She continued to vigorously dry Asher's silky coat before exchanging the damp thermal blanket for a dry one and then turning to Jax to help him get dry before giving him another blanket.

"I owe you big time," said Nicole. "Don't think I don't know it. I owe you a debt I can never repay."

The Kodiak snuffled her hand again as Kyra crested the bank of the river. "That's the Kodiak way to say thanks. It looks like you've got things well in hand."

"Judith?"

"Deader than the proverbial doornail. Her body feels like ice. My guess is she inhaled some of the ice water so didn't last long. Asher's swipe didn't penetrate her clothes to the skin, but it doesn't matter as Doc is our medical examiner. There's no way he'd let his findings incriminate Jax or Ash, but in this case, I don't think he'll have to worry about it. Do you know why?"

"Money. She was getting another divorce and would have had to split her earnings from the company with her ex. With me out of the way she gets her half of her community property and then my profit split." Nicole shook her head. "She always did say she gave everything for her business. It seems she was right."

Kyra took over helping Jax while Nicole returned

to Asher. Once both men were warmed and relatively dry, they shifted back, which seemed to help with both. They each got redressed and then went down to wrap Judith's body in a tarp and pull it up away from the river. When Jax returned, he called back to Doc and asked him to come retrieve the body.

Jax broke out the emergency heating packs to help stave off the cold until Doc arrived with a sled attached to his snowmobile. They lifted Judith's corpse into a body bag and then secured it to the back of the sled. Once done, Doc headed back to town while the four of them returned to the gazebo to pick up the snowmobiles that had been left there.

Later that night, tucked into the warm bed at the little cottage, Nicole lay tied to Asher, impaled on his knot in a post-coital haze. In spite of all that happened earlier in the day, everything seemed damn close to perfect.

Asher was lying with one arm behind his head, showcasing his muscular bicep. "What are you thinking?"

"Not much. I suppose I should be, but I'm not. I'm just kind of drifting."

"Drifting is good," he rumbled softly, kissing her.

"I thought I'd lost you."

"Never happen. I waited a long time to find you. I have no intention of not spending the rest of my life just like this."

Nicole laughed. "You might find it difficult to do your job with me tied to you."

"Maybe, but I'm willing to try it if you are."

He rubbed her back, lightly skimming her backside. It was fascinating to her that those same hands that were bringing comfort could also arouse her so intensely and bring her discipline and pain when needed. She rubbed her cheek against his chest and allowed the tension to fade away until she was completely relaxed as she snuggled against him.

"What did the lawyer say when you spoke with her?"

"She thought it was incredibly generous that we were willing to just write off Judith's death as an accident with no reference to her having tried to kill me. She said she wished she could be more shocked that Judith had done what she did. She thought given that I was remaining up here that closing the business was probably the easiest and cleanest way to do it."

"What happens to Judith's now widower?"

"Poppy was downright maniacal. She said all he'll get is all of Judith's personal property. Because of our agreement, all of the business assets go to me as the surviving partner. So, there will be more than enough money to get things going up here."

Asher's breathing deepened as he descended into the land of nod, and Nicole realized how fiercely she loved the wolf who had saved her not only from freezing to death or being murdered by her former business partner, but from herself and never truly embracing herself and her own talents. There were those who said a woman couldn't have it all. They were wrong. She would have it all and then some. With a soft smile playing about her lips, she closed her eyes, content to join Asher in the land of dreams—both sleeping and waking.

EPILOGUE

There were times Jax missed having Kyra as his lover, but he knew that wasn't fair to either of them. Their time together had been finite; they'd always known that. As he rose from his bed, the images of the woman with the tawny hair kissed by the sun flooded his brain. When she had first appeared two years ago, Jax had known she was his fated mate. He didn't tell anyone about the dreams—they would have scoffed at him.

Especially Asher. At that time, Asher didn't believe the tales his kind told of fated mates and that to be complete, one needed to find her so they could share their destiny. Jax smiled. He was certain now that if he told Asher about the visions that continued to strengthen and show up more regularly, his friend would tell him to do whatever he had to in order to find her and bring her home.

Bears were more solitary creatures and while their legends included myths about a fated mate, it wasn't as compelling a need as it was for the more socialized pack status of wolves. He envied his friend his fated mate. Nicole had brought about a huge change in Asher. She had defrosted a heart that he had allowed winter to settle in. Could a fated mate of his own do the same for him?

Jax snorted. Such romantic drivel was best left to wolf-shifters and the equally passionate lynx-shifters. Most shifters, like the bear-shifters, followed a more individualized path and married for more practical reasons.

But what if Asher was right? What if Jax's fated mate was out there, just waiting for him to find her and save them both from a life of quiet desperation?

Want to know Jax's story? Click Here to read how he meets Autumn.

The first time she saw him he was coming out of the river... Oh! what a view.

Jackson Miller (Jax) left the SEALs to return to his small hometown, Mystic River, Alaska where all the residents are shifters. He's a grumpy bear shifter and the sheriff.

Autumn Bradley was hiking with her fiancé for a birthday weekend. When he decides Alaska is a bit too rustic for his tastes, he leaves Autumn behind to hike out by herself. Unknowingly taking the sat phone, compass and GPS with him, leaving Autumn without directional assistance in the path of a snowstorm.

Once the rangers discover one of the hikers has failed to return to the base camp, they call in the best tracker they know… Jax. He is not exactly happy to go out in the bad weather to track down the irresponsible woman. Learning she is his fated mate was rather shocking.

Even if they make it out of the storm will she ever be accepted in his small town of shifters?

Come visit Mystic River, Alaska a small, remote town that has always been a safe community for different types of shifters. These shifters are gorgeous, possessive and finding their fated mate is high on their priority list.

Take a walk on the wild side with these curvy heroines, their sexy fated mates and scenes that sizzle.

BONUS SCENE

I have an **EXCLUSIVE** bonus scene as a thank you! All you have to do is click the link below, sign up for my newsletter, and you'll get an email giving you access!

SIGN UP HERE

<u>Wild Fire</u>

<u>Dark Fire</u>

Mystic River Shifters (small town shifter)

<u>Defiant Mate</u>

<u>Savage Mate</u>

<u>Reckless Mate</u>

<u>Shameless Mate</u>

<u>Runaway Mate</u>

<u>Stolen Mate</u>

<u>Bah Humbug Mate</u>

<u>Hidden Mate</u>

<u>Unforeseen Mate</u>

<u>Shadow Mate</u>

<u>Book Set Vol. 1</u>

<u>Book Set Vol. 2</u>

<u>Book Set Vol. 3</u>

Otter Cover Shifters (small town shifters/ spinoff Mystic River)

<u>Suspicious Mate</u>

<u>Unexpected Mate</u>

<u>Substitute Mate</u>

<u>Accidental Mate</u>

Feral Mate

Mystic Mate

Elusive Mate

Mysterious Mate

Syndicate Masters

Midwest

Kiss of Luck

Stroke of Fortune

Twist of Fate

Eastern Seaboard

High Stakes

High Roller

High Bet

La Cosa Nostra

Ruthless Honor

Feral Oath

Defiant Vow

Northern Lights

Alliance

Complication

Judgment

Syndicate Masters

The Bargain

The Pact

The Agreement

The Understanding

The Pledge

Box Set

Looking Glass Multiverse

Shifted Reality

Shifted Existence

Shifted Dimension

Box Set

Reign of Fire

Dragon Storm

Dragon Roar

Dragon Fury

Masters of Valor (spin off Masters of the Savoy)

Prophecy

Illusion

Deception

Inheritance

Masters of the Savoy

Advance

Negotiation

Submission

Contract

Bound

Release

Ghost Cat Canyon

Determined

Untamed

Bold

Fearless

Strong

Fated Legacy (spin-off Tangled Vines)

Touch of Fate

Touch of Darkness

Touch of Light

Touch of Fire

Touch of Ice

Touch of Destiny

Tangled Vines (spin-off Wayward Mates)

Corked

Uncorked

Decanted

Breathe

Full Bodied

Late Harvest

Mulled Wine

Wayward Mates

Carriage House (spinoff Club Southside)

Viktor

Club Southside (spinoff Mercenary Masters)

The Scoundrel

The Scavenger

The Rookie

The Sentinel

The Keeper

The Enforcer

The Player

Mercenary Masters

Devil Dog

Alpha Dog

Bull Dog

Top Dog

Big Dog

Sea Dog

Ice Dog

Mystery, She Wrote

Invitation To Murder

Murder Before Dawn

Hook, Line and Mystery

Paint Me A Murder

Deadline To Murder

Relentless Pursuit (Duet)

To Love a Thief

My Fair Thief

Charade

Wild Mustang

Hampton

Mac

Croft

Noah

Thom

Reid

Crooked Creek Ranch

Taming His Cowgirl

Tamed on the Ranch

Co-writes

Masters of the Deep

Silent Predator

Fierce Predator

Savage Predator

Wicked Predator

Deadly Predator

ABOUT DELTA JAMES

Other books by Delta James: <u>https://www.</u> <u>deltajames.com/</u>

As a USA Today bestselling romance author, Delta James aims to captivate readers with stories about complex heroines and the dominant alpha males who adore them. For Delta, romance is more than just a love story; it's a journey with challenges and thrills along the way.

After creating a second chapter for herself that was dramatically different than the first, Delta now resides in Florida where she relaxes on warm summer evenings with her loveable pack of basset hounds as they watch the birds, squirrels and lizards. When not crafting fast-paced tales, she enjoys horseback riding, walks on the beach, and white-water rafting.

Her readers mean the world to her, and Delta tries to interact personally to as many messages as she can. If you'd like to chat or discuss books, you can find Delta on Instagram, Facebook, and in her private reader group https://www.facebook.com/groups/ 348982795738444.

Keep up with Delta on Social Media

<u>Facebook page</u>

<u>Facebook group</u>

<u>Instagram</u>

<u>TikTok</u>

<u>Bookbub</u>

<u>Goodreads</u>

<u>Patreon</u>

<u>Signup</u> for my newsletter and

Get the good stuff...
Each month Delta shares her writing updates, novel releases, exclusive content and some fun personal stories.
Plus - there's often a giveaway!

Thank you!

ACKNOWLEDGMENTS

Thank you to my Patreon supporters.
I couldn't do this without you!

Carol Chase
Latoya McBride
Julia Rappaport
D F
Ellen
Margaret Bloodworth
Tamara Crooks
Rhonda
Autumn
Suzy Sawkins
Cindy Vernon
Linda Kniffen-Wager
Karen Somerville